The Old Man and the Sea

原著雙語彩圖本

海明威（Ernest Hemingway）■著　黛孜■譯

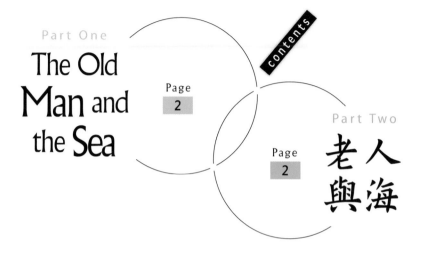

Part One

The Old Man and the Sea

Page
2

contents

Part Two

Page
2

老人與海

The Old
Man and
the Sea

He was an old man who fished alone in a skiff in the Gulf Stream and he had gone eighty-four days now without taking a fish. In the first forty days a boy had been with him. But after forty days without a fish the boy's parents had told him that the old man was now definitely and finally *salao*†, which is the worst form of unlucky, and the boy had gone at their orders in another boat which caught three good fish the first week. It made the boy sad to see the old man come in each day with his skiff empty and he always went down to help him carry either the coiled lines or the gaff and harpoon and the sail that was furled around the mast. The sail was patched with flour sacks and, furled, it looked like the flag of permanent defeat.

The old man was thin and gaunt with deep wrinkles in the back of his neck. The brown blotches of the benevolent skin cancer the sun brings from its reflection on the tropic

† (Spanish) unlucky

sea were on his cheeks. The blotches ran well down the sides of his face and his hands had the deep-creased scars from handling heavy fish on the cords. But none of these scars were fresh. They were as old as erosions in a fishless desert.

Everything about him was old except his eyes and they were the same color as the sea and were cheerful and undefeated.

"Santiago," the boy said to him as they climbed the bank from where the skiff was hauled up. "I could go with you again. We've made some money."

The old man had taught the boy to fish and the boy loved him.

"No," the old man said. "You're with a lucky boat. Stay with them."

"But remember how you went eighty-seven days without fish and then we caught big ones every day for three weeks."

"I remember," the old man said. "I know you did not leave me because you doubted."

"It was papa made me leave. I am a boy and I must obey him."

"I know," the old man said. "It is quite normal."

"He hasn't much faith."

"No," the old man said. "But we have. Haven't we?"

"Yes," the boy said. "Can I offer you a beer on the Terrace and then we'll take the stuff home."

"Why not?" the old man said. "Between fishermen."

They sat on the Terrace and many of the fishermen made fun of the old man and he was not angry. Others, of the older fishermen, looked at him and were sad. But they did not show it and they spoke politely about the current and the depths they had drifted their lines at and the steady good weather and of what they had seen.

The successful fishermen of that day were already in and had butchered their marlin out and carried them laid full length across two planks, with two men staggering at the end of each plank, to the fish house where they waited for the ice truck to carry them to the market in Havana. Those who had caught sharks had taken them to the shark factory on the other side of the cove where they were hoisted on a block and tackle, their livers removed, their fins cut off and their hides skinned out and their flesh cut into strips for salting.

When the wind was in the east a smell came across the harbor from the shark factory; but today there was only the faint edge of the odor because the wind had backed into the north and then dropped off and it was pleasant and sunny on the Terrace.

"Santiago," the boy said.

"Yes," the old man said. He was holding his glass and thinking of many years ago.

"Can I go out to get sardines for you for tomorrow?"

"No. Go and play baseball. I can still row and Rogelio will throw the net."

"I would like to go. If I cannot fish with you, I would like to serve in some way."

"You bought me a beer," the old man said. "You are already a man."

"How old was I when you first took me in a boat?"

"Five and you nearly were killed when I brought the fish in too green and he nearly tore the boat to pieces. Can you remember?"

"I can remember the tail slapping and banging and the thwart breaking and the noise of the clubbing. I can remember you throwing me into the bow where the wet coiled lines were and feeling the whole boat shiver and the noise of you clubbing him like chopping a tree down and the sweet blood smell all over me."

"Can you really remember that or did I just tell it to you?"

"I remember everything from when we first went together."

The old man looked at him with his sun-burned, confident loving eyes.

"If you were my boy I'd take you out and gamble," he said. "But you are your father's and your mother's and you are in a lucky boat."

"May I get the sardines? I know where I can get four baits too."

"I have mine left from today. I put them in salt in the box."

"Let me get four fresh ones."

"One," the old man said. His hope and his confidence had never gone. But now they were freshening as when the breeze rises.

"Two," the boy said.

"Two," the old man agreed. "You didn't steal them?"

"I would," the boy said. "But I bought these."

"Thank you," the old man said. He was too simple to wonder when he had attained humility. But he knew he had attained it and he knew it was not disgraceful and it carried no loss of true pride.

"Tomorrow is going to be a good day with this current," he said.

"Where are you going?" the boy asked.

"Far out to come in when the wind shifts. I want to be out before it is light."

"I'll try to get him to work far out," the boy said. "Then if you hook something truly big we can come to your aid."

"He does not like to work too far out."

"No," the boy said. "But I will see something that he cannot see such as a bird working and get him to come out after dolphin."

"Are his eyes that bad?"

"He is almost blind."

"It is strange," the old man said. "He never went turtl-ing. That is what kills the eyes."

"But you went turtle-ing for years off the Mosquito Coast and your eyes are good."

"I am a strange old man"

"But are you strong enough now for a truly big fish?"

"I think so. And there are many tricks."

"Let us take the stuff home," the boy said. "So I can get the cast net and go after the sardines."

They picked up the gear from the boat. The old man carried the mast on his shoulder and the boy carried the wooden box with the coiled, hard-braided brown lines, the gaff and the harpoon with its shaft. The box with the baits was under the stern of the skiff along with the club that was used to subdue the big fish when they were brought alongside. No one would steal from the old man but it was better to take the sail and the heavy lines home as the dew was bad for them and, though he was quite sure no local people would steal from him, the old man thought that a gaff and a harpoon were needless temptations to leave in a boat.

They walked up the road together to the old man's shack and went in through its open door. The old man leaned the mast with its wrapped sail against the wall and the boy put the box and the other gear beside it. The mast was nearly as long as the one room of the shack. The shack was made of the

tough budshields of the royal palm which are called *guano*
and in it there was a bed, a table, one chair, and a place on
the dirt floor to cook with charcoal. On the brown walls
of the flattened, overlapping leaves of the sturdy fibered
guano there was a picture in color of the Sacred Heart of
Jesus and another of the Virgin of Cobre[†]. These were
relics of his wife. Once there had been a tinted photograph
of his wife on the wall but he had taken it down because it
made him too lonely to see it and it was on the shelf in the
corner under his clean shirt.

"What do you have to eat?" the boy asked.

"A pot of yellow rice with fish. Do you want some?"

"No. I will eat at home. Do you want me to make the
fire?"

"No. I will make it later on. Or I may eat the rice cold."

"May I take the cast net?"

"Of course."

[†] Our Lady of Charity, the most
venerated in all of Cuba

There was no cast net and the boy remembered when they had sold it. But they went through this fiction every day. There was no pot of yellow rice and fish and the boy knew this too.

"Eighty-five is a lucky number," the old man said. "How would you like to see me bring one in that dressed out over a thousand pounds?"

"I'll get the cast net and go for sardines. Will you sit in the sun in the doorway?"

"Yes. I have yesterday's paper and I will read the baseball."

The boy did not know whether yesterday's paper was a fiction too. But the old man brought it out from under the bed.

"Perico gave it to me at the *bodega*†," he explained.

"I'll be back when I have the sardines. I'll keep yours and mine together on ice and we can share them in the morning. When I come back you can tell me about the baseball."

"The Yankees cannot lose."

"But I fear the Indians of Cleveland."

"Have faith in the Yankees my son. Think of the great DiMaggio."

"I fear both the Tigers of Detroit and the Indians of Cleveland."

"Be careful or you will fear even the Reds of Cincinnati and the White Sox of Chicago."

"You study it and tell me when I come back."

"Do you think we should buy a terminal of the lottery with an eighty-five? Tomorrow is the eighty-fifth day."

"We can do that," the boy said. "But what about the eighty-seven of your great record?"

"It could not happen twice. Do you think you can find an eighty-five?"

"I can order one."

"One sheet. That's two dollars and a half. Who can we borrow that from?"

"That's easy. I can always borrow two dollars and a half."

"I think perhaps I can too. But I try not to borrow. First you borrow. Then you beg."

"Keep warm old man," the boy said. "Remember we are in September."

"The month when the great fish come," the old man said. "Anyone can be a fisherman in May."

"I go now for the sardines," the boy said.

† (Spanish) small store

When the boy came back the old man was asleep in the chair and the sun was down. The boy took the old army blanket off the bed and spread it over the back of the chair and over the old man's shoulders. They were strange shoulders, still powerful although very old, and the neck was still strong too and the creases did not show so much when the old man was asleep and his head fallen forward. His shirt had been patched so many times that it was like the sail and the patches were faded to many different shades by the sun. The old man's head was very old though and with his eyes closed there was no life in his face. The newspaper lay across his knees and the weight of his arm held it there in the evening breeze. He was barefooted.

The boy left him there and when he came back the old man was still asleep.

"Wake up old man," the boy said and put his hand on one of the old man's knees.

The old man opened his eyes and for a moment he was coming back from a long way away. Then he smiled.

"What have you got?" he asked.

"Supper," said the boy. "We're going to have supper."

"I'm not very hungry."

"Come on and eat. You can't fish and not eat."

"I have," the old man said getting up and taking the newspaper and folding it. Then he started to fold the blanket.

"Keep the blanket around you," the boy said. "You'll not

fish without eating while I'm alive."

"Then live a long time and take care of yourself," the old man said. "What are we eating?"

"Black beans and rice, fried bananas, and some stew."

The boy had brought them in a two-decker metal container from the Terrace. The two sets of knives and forks and spoons were in his pocket with a paper napkin wrapped around each set.

"Who gave this to you?"

"Martin. The owner."

"I must thank him."

"I thanked him already," the boy said. "You don't need to thank him."

"I'll give him the belly meat of a big fish," the old man said. "Has he done this for us more than once?"

"I think so."

"I must give him something more than the belly meat then. He is very thoughtful for us."

"He sent two beers."

"I like the beer in cans best."

"I know. But this is in bottles, Hatuey beer, and I take back the bottles."

"That's very kind of you," the old man said. "Should we eat?"

"I've been asking you to," the boy told him gently. "I have not wished to open the container until you were ready."

"I'm ready now," the old man said. "I only needed time to wash."

Where did you wash? the boy thought. The village water

supply was two streets down the road. I must have water here for him, the boy thought, and soap and a good towel. Why am I so thoughtless? I must get him another shirt and a jacket for the winter and some sort of shoes and another blanket.

"Your stew is excellent," the old man said.

"Tell me about the baseball," the boy asked him.

"In the American League it is the Yankees as I said," the old man said happily.

"They lost today," the boy told him.

"That means nothing. The great DiMaggio is himself again."

"They have other men on the team."

"Naturally. But he makes the difference. In the other league, between Brooklyn and Philadelphia I must take Brooklyn. But then I think of Dick Sisler and those great drives in the old park."

"There was nothing ever like them. He hits the longest ball I have ever seen."

"Do you remember when he used to come to the Terrace? I wanted to take him fishing but I was too timid to ask him. Then I asked you to ask him and you were too timid."

"I know. It was a great mistake. He might have gone with us. Then we would have that for all of our lives."

"I would like to take the great DiMaggio fishing," the old man said. "They say his father was a fisherman. Maybe he was as poor as we are and would understand."

"The great Sisler's father was never poor and he, the father, was playing in the Big Leagues when he was my age."

"When I was your age I was before the mast on a square rigged ship that ran to Africa and I have seen lions on the beaches in the evening."

"I know. You told me."

"Should we talk about Africa or about baseball?"

"Baseball I think," the boy said. "Tell me about the great John J. McGraw." He said *Jota* for J.

"He used to come to the Terrace sometimes too in the older days. But he was rough and harsh-spoken and difficult when he was drinking. His mind was on horses as well as baseball. At least he carried lists of horses at all times in his pocket and frequently spoke the names of horses on the telephone."

"He was a great manager," the boy said. "My father thinks he was the greatest."

"Because he came here the most times," the old man said. "If Durocher had continued to come here each year your father would think him the greatest manager."

"Who is the greatest manager, really, Luque or Mike Gonzalez?"

"I think they are equal."

"And the best fisherman is you."

"No. I know others better."

"*Qué va*[†]," the boy said. "There are many good fishermen and some great ones. But there is only you."

"Thank you. You make me happy. I hope no fish will come along so great that he will prove us wrong."

"There is no such fish if you are still strong as you say."

"I may not be as strong as I think," the old man said. "But I know many tricks and I have resolution."

"You ought to go to bed now so that you will be fresh in the morning. I will take the things back to the Terrace."

"Good night then. I will wake you in the morning."

"You're my alarm clock," the boy said.

"Age is my alarm clock," the old man said. "Why do old men wake so early? Is it to have one longer day?"

"I don't know," the boy said. "All I know is that young boys sleep late and hard."

"I can remember it," the old man said. "I'll waken you in time."

"I do not like for him to waken me. It is as though I were inferior."

[†] (Spanish) No way.

"I know."

"Sleep well old man."

The boy went out. They had eaten with no light on the table and the old man took off his trousers and went to bed in the dark. He rolled his trousers up to make a pillow, putting the newspaper inside them. He rolled himself in the blanket and slept on the other old newspapers that covered the springs of the bed.

He was asleep in a short time and he dreamed of Africa when he was a boy and the long golden beaches and the white beaches, so white they hurt your eyes, and the high capes and the great brown mountains. He lived along that coast now every night and in his dreams he heard the surf roar and saw the native boats come riding through it. He smelled the tar and oakum of the deck as he slept and he

smelled the smell of Africa that the land breeze brought at morning.

Usually when he smelled the land breeze he woke up and dressed to go and wake the boy. But tonight the smell of the land breeze came very early and he knew it was too early in his dream and went on dreaming to see the white peaks of the Islands rising from the sea and then he dreamed of the different harbors and roadsteads of the Canary Islands.

He no longer dreamed of storms, nor of women, nor of great occurrences, nor of great fish, nor fights, nor contests of strength, nor of his wife. He only dreamed of places now and of the lions on the beach. They played like young cats in the dusk and he loved them as he loved the boy. He never dreamed about the boy. He simply woke, looked out the open door at the moon and unrolled his trousers and put them on. He urinated outside the shack and then went

up the road to wake the boy. He was shivering with the morning cold. But he knew he would shiver himself warm and that soon he would be rowing.

The door of the house where the boy lived was unlocked and he opened it and walked in quietly with his bare feet. The boy was asleep on a cot in the first room and the old man could see him clearly with the light that came in from the dying moon. He took hold of one foot gently and held it until the boy woke and turned and looked at him. The old man nodded and the boy took his trousers from the chair by the bed and, sitting on the bed, pulled them on.

The old man went out the door and the boy came after him. He was sleepy and the old man put his arm across his shoulders and said, "I am sorry."

"*Qué va,*" the boy said. "It is what a man must do."

They walked down the road to the old man's shack and all along the road, in the dark, barefoot men were moving, carrying the masts of their boats.

When they reached the old man's shack the boy took the rolls of line in the basket and the harpoon and gaff and the old man carried the mast with the furled sail on his shoulder.

"Do you want coffee?" the boy asked.

"We'll put the gear in the boat and then get some."

They had coffee from condensed milk cans at an early morning place that served fishermen.

"How did you sleep old man?" the boy asked. He was waking up now although it was still hard for him to leave his sleep.

"Very well, Manolin," the old man said. "I feel confident today."

"So do I," the boy said. "Now I must get your sardines and mine and your fresh baits. He brings our gear himself. He never wants anyone to carry anything."

"We're different," the old man said. "I let you carry things when you were five years old."

"I know it," the boy said. "I'll be right back. Have another coffee. We have credit here."

He walked off, barefooted on the coral rocks, to the ice house where the baits were stored.

The old man drank his coffee slowly. It was all he would have all day and he knew that he should take it. For a long time now eating had bored him and he never carried a lunch. He had a bottle of water in the bow of the skiff and that was all he needed for the day.

The boy was back now with the sardines and the two baits wrapped in a newspaper and they went down the trail to the skiff, feeling the pebbled sand under their feet, and lifted the skiff and slid her into the water.

"Good luck old man."

"Good luck," the old man said. He fitted the rope lashings of the oars onto the thole pins and, leaning forward against the thrust of the blades in the water, he began to row out of the harbor in the dark. There were other boats from the other beaches going out to sea and the old man heard the dip and push of their oars even though he could not see them now the moon was below the hills.

Sometimes someone would speak in a boat. But most of the boats were silent except for the dip of the oars. They spread apart after they were out of the mouth of the harbor and each one headed for the part of the ocean where he hoped to find fish. The old man knew he was going far out and he left the smell of the land behind and rowed out into the clean early morning smell of the ocean. He saw the phosphorescence of the Gulf weed in the water as he rowed over the part of the ocean that the fishermen called the great well because there was a sudden deep of seven hundred fathoms where all sorts of fish congregated because of the swirl the current made against the steep walls of the floor of the ocean. Here there were concentrations of shrimp and bait fish and sometimes schools of squid in the deepest holes and these rose close to the surface at night where all the wandering fish fed on them.

In the dark the old man could feel the morning coming and as he rowed he heard the trembling sound as flying fish left the water and the hissing that their stiff set wings made as they soared away in the darkness. He was very fond of flying fish as they were his principal friends on the ocean. He was sorry for the birds, especially the small delicate dark terns that were always flying and looking and almost never finding, and he thought, the birds have a harder life than we do except for the robber birds and the heavy strong ones. Why did they make birds so delicate and fine as those sea swallows when the ocean can be so cruel? She is kind and very beautiful. But she can be so cruel and it comes so suddenly and such birds that fly, dipping and hunting, with their small sad voices are made too delicately for the sea.

He always thought of the sea as *la mar*[†] which is what people call her in Spanish when they love her. Sometimes those who love her say bad things of her but they are always said as though she were a woman. Some of the younger fishermen, those who used buoys as floats for

their lines and had motorboats, bought when the shark livers had brought much money, spoke of her as *el mar*† which is masculine. They spoke of her as a contestant or a place or even an enemy. But the old man always thought of her as feminine and as something that gave or withheld great favors, and if she did wild or wicked things it was because she could not help them. The moon affects her as it does a woman, he thought.

He was rowing steadily and it was no effort for him since he kept well within his speed and the surface of the ocean was flat except for the occasional swirls of the current. He was letting the current do a third of the work and as it started to be light he saw he was already further out than he had hoped to be at this hour.

I worked the deep wells for a week and did nothing, he thought. Today I'll work out where the schools of bonito and albacore are and maybe there will be a big one with

† (Spanish) *la mar*: feminine
† (Spanish) *el mar*: masculine

them. Before it was really light he had his baits out and was drifting with the current. One bait was down forty fathoms. The second was at seventy-five and the third and fourth were down in the blue water at one hundred and one hundred and twenty-five fathoms. Each bait hung head down with the shank of the hook inside the bait fish, tied and sewed solid and all the projecting part of the hook, the curve and the point, was covered with fresh sardines. Each sardine was hooked through both eyes so that they made a half-garland on the projecting steel. There was no part of the hook that a great fish could feel which was not sweet smelling and good tasting.

The boy had given him two fresh small tunas, or albacores, which hung on the two deepest lines like plummets and, on the others, he had a big blue runner and a yellow jack that had been used before; but they were in good condition still and had the excellent sardines to give them scent and attractiveness. Each line, as thick around as a big pencil, was looped onto a green-sapped stick so that any pull or touch on the bait would make the stick dip and each line had two forty-fathom coils which could be made fast to the other spare coils so that, if it were necessary, a fish could take out over three hundred fathoms of line.

Now the man watched the dip of the three sticks over the side of the skiff and rowed gently to keep the lines straight up and down and at their proper depths. It was quite light and any moment now the sun would rise.

The sun rose thinly from the sea and the old man could see the other boats, low on the water and well in toward the shore, spread out across the current. Then the sun was brighter and the glare came on the water and then, as it rose clear, the flat sea sent it back at his eyes so that it hurt sharply and he rowed without looking into it. He looked down into the water and watched the lines that went straight down into the dark of the water. He kept them straighter than anyone did, so that at each level in the darkness of the stream there would be a bait waiting exactly where he wished it to be for any fish that swam there. Others let them drift with the current and sometimes they were at sixty fathoms when the fishermen thought they were at a hundred.

But, he thought, I keep them with precision. Only I have no luck anymore. But who knows? Maybe today. Every day is a new day. It is better to be lucky. But I would rather be exact. Then when luck comes you are ready.

The sun was two hours higher now and it did not hurt his eyes so much to look into the east. There were only three boats in sight now and they showed very low and far inshore.

All my life the early sun has hurt my eyes, he thought. Yet they are still good. In the evening I can look straight into it without getting the blackness. It has more force in the evening too. But in the morning it is painful.

Just then he saw a man-of-war bird with his long black wings circling in the sky ahead of him. He made a quick

drop, slanting down on his back-swept wings, and then circled again.

"He's got something," the old man said aloud. "He's not just looking."

He rowed slowly and steadily toward where the bird was circling. He did not hurry and he kept his lines straight up and down. But he crowded the current a little so that he was still fishing correctly though faster than he would have fished if he was not trying to use the bird.

The bird went higher in the air and circled again, his wings motionless. Then he dove suddenly and the old man saw flying fish spurt out of the water and sail desperately over the surface.

"Dolphin," the old man said aloud. "Big dolphin."

He shipped his oars and brought a small line from under the bow. It had a wire leader and a medium-sized hook and he baited it with one of the sardines. He let it go over the side and then made it fast to a ring bolt in the stern. Then he baited another line and left it coiled in the shade of the bow. He went back to rowing and to watching the long-winged black bird who was working, now, low over the water.

As he watched the bird dipped again slanting his wings for the dive and then swinging them wildly and ineffectually as he followed the flying fish. The old man could see the slight bulge in the water that the big dolphin raised as they followed the escaping fish. The dolphin were cutting through the water below the flight of the fish and would be in the water, driving at speed, when the fish dropped. It is a big school of dolphin, he thought. They are widespread and the flying fish have little chance. The bird has no chance. The flying fish are too big for him and they go too fast.

He watched the flying fish burst out again and again and the ineffectual movements of the bird. That school has gotten away from me, he thought. They are moving out too fast and too far. But perhaps I will pick up a stray and perhaps my big fish is around them. My big fish must be somewhere.

The clouds over the land now rose like mountains and the coast was only a long green line with the gray blue hills behind it. The water was a dark blue now, so dark that it was almost purple. As he looked down into it he saw the red sifting of the plankton in the dark water and the strange light the sun made now. He watched his lines to see them go straight down out of sight into the water and he was happy to see so much plankton because it meant fish. The strange light the sun made in the water, now that the sun was higher, meant good weather and so did the shape of the clouds over the land. But the bird was almost out of sight now and nothing showed on the surface of the water but some patches of yellow, sun-bleached Sargasso weed and the purple, formalized, iridescent, gelatinous bladder of a Portuguese man-of-war floating close beside the boat. It turned on its side and then righted itself. It floated cheerfully as a bubble with its long deadly purple filaments trailing a yard behind it in the water.

"*Agua mala*," the man said. "You whore."

From where he swung lightly against his oars he looked down into the water and saw the tiny fish that were colored like the trailing filaments and swam between them and under the small shade the bubble made as it drifted. They were immune to its poison. But men were not and when some of the filaments would catch on a line and rest there slimy and purple while the old man was working a fish, he would have

welts and sores on his arms and hands of the sort that poison ivy or poison oak can give. But these poisonings from the *agua mala* came quickly and struck like a whiplash.

The iridescent bubbles were beautiful. But they were the falsest thing in the sea and the old man loved to see the big sea turtles eating them. The turtles saw them, approached them from the front, then shut their eyes so they were completely carapaced and ate them filaments and all. The old man loved to see the turtles eat them and he loved to walk on them on the beach after a storm and hear them pop when he stepped on them with the horny soles of his feet.

He loved green turtles and hawk-bills with their elegance and speed and their great value and he had a friendly contempt for the huge, stupid loggerheads, yellow in their armor-plating, strange in their love-making, and happily eating the Portuguese men-of-war with their eyes shut.

He had no mysticism about turtles although he had gone in turtle boats for many years. He was sorry for them all, even the great trunk backs that were as long as the skiff and weighed a ton. Most people are heartless about turtles because a turtle's heart will beat for hours after he has been cut up and butchered. But the old man thought, I have such a heart too and my feet and hands are like theirs. He ate the white eggs to give himself strength. He ate them all through May to be strong in September and October for the truly big fish.

He also drank a cup of shark liver oil each day from the big drum in the shack where many of the fishermen kept their gear. It was there for all fishermen who wanted it. Most fishermen hated the taste. But it was no worse than getting up at the hours that they rose and it was very good against all colds and grippes and it was good for the eyes.

Now the old man looked up and saw that the bird was circling again.

"He's found fish," he said aloud. No flying fish broke the surface and there was no scattering of bait fish. But as the old man watched, a small tuna rose in the air, turned and dropped head first into the water. The tuna shone silver in the sun and after he had dropped back into the water another and another rose and they were jumping in all directions, churning the water and leaping in long jumps after the bait. They were circling it and driving it.

If they don't travel too fast I will get into them, the old man thought, and he watched the school working the water white and the bird now dropping and dipping into the bait fish that were forced to the surface in their panic.

"The bird is a great help," the old man said. Just then the stern line came taut under his foot, where he had kept a loop

of the line, and he dropped his oars and felt the weight of the small tuna's shivering pull as he held the line firm and commenced to haul it in. The shivering increased as he pulled in and he could see the blue back of the fish in the water and the gold of his sides before he swung him over the side and into the boat. He lay in the stern in the sun, compact and bullet shaped, his big, unintelligent eyes staring as he thumped his life out against the planking of the boat with the quick shivering strokes of his neat, fast-moving tail. The old man hit him on the head for kindness and kicked him, his body still shuddering, under the shade of the stern.

"Albacore," he said aloud. "He'll make a beautiful bait. He'll weigh ten pounds."

He did not remember when he had first started to talk aloud when he was by himself. He had sung when he was by himself in the old days and he had sung at night sometimes when he was alone steering on his watch in the smacks or in the turtle boats. He had probably started to talk aloud, when alone, when the boy had left. But he did not remember. When he and the boy fished together they usually spoke only when it was necessary. They talked at night or when they were storm-bound by bad weather. It was considered a virtue not to talk unnecessarily at sea and the old man had always considered it so and respected it. But now he said his thoughts aloud many times since there was no one that they could annoy.

"If the others heard me talking out loud they would think that I am crazy," he said aloud. "But since I am not crazy, I do not care. And the rich have radios to talk to them in their boats and to bring them the baseball."

Now is no time to think of baseball, he thought. Now is the time to think of only one thing. That which I was born for. There might be a big one around that school, he thought. I picked up only a straggler from the albacore that were feeding. But they are working far out and fast. Everything that shows on the surface today travels very fast and to the north-east. Can that be the time of day? Or is it some sign of weather that I do not know?

He could not see the green of the shore now but only the tops of the blue hills that showed white as though they were snow-capped and the clouds that looked like high snow mountains above them. The sea was very dark and the light made prisms in the water. The myriad flecks of the plankton were annulled now by the high sun and it was only the great deep prisms in the blue water that the old man saw now with his lines going straight down into the water that was a mile deep.

The tuna, the fishermen called all the fish of that species tuna and only distinguished among them by their proper names when they came to sell them or to trade them for baits, were down again. The sun was hot now and the old man felt it on the back of his neck and felt the sweat trickle down his back as he rowed.

I could just drift, he thought, and sleep and put a bight of line around my toe to wake me. But today is eighty-five days and I should fish the day well.

Just then, watching his lines, he saw one of the projecting green sticks dip sharply.

"Yes," he said. "Yes," and shipped his oars without bumping the boat. He reached out for the line and held it softly between the thumb and forefinger of his right hand. He felt no strain nor weight and he held the line lightly. Then it came again. This time it was a tentative pull, not solid nor heavy, and he knew exactly what it was. One hundred fathoms down a marlin was eating the sardines that covered the point and the shank of the hook where the hand-forged hook projected from the head of the small tuna.

The old man held the line delicately, and softly, with his left hand, unleashed it from the stick. Now he could let it run through his fingers without the fish feeling any tension.

This far out, he must be huge in this month, he thought. Eat them, fish. Eat them. Please eat them. How fresh they are and you down there six hundred feet in that cold water in the dark. Make another turn in the dark and come back and eat them.

He felt the light delicate pulling and then a harder pull when a sardine's head must have been more difficult to break from the hook. Then there was nothing.

"Come on," the old man said aloud. "Make another turn. Just smell them. Aren't they lovely? Eat them good now and

then there is the tuna. Hard and cold and lovely. Don't be shy, fish. Eat them."

He waited with the line between his thumb and his finger, watching it and the other lines at the same time for the fish might have swum up or down. Then came the same delicate pulling touch again.

"He'll take it," the old man said aloud. "God help him to take it."

He did not take it though. He was gone and the old man felt nothing.

"He can't have gone," he said. "Christ knows he can't have gone. He's making a turn. Maybe he has been hooked before and he remembers something of it."

Then he felt the gentle touch on the line and he was happy.

"It was only his turn," he said. "He'll take it."

He was happy feeling the gentle pulling and then he felt something hard and unbelievably heavy. It was the weight of the fish and he let the line slip down, down, down, unrolling off the first of the two reserve coils. As it went down, slipping lightly through the old man's fingers, he still could feel the great weight, though the pressure of his thumb and finger were almost imperceptible.

"What a fish," he said. "He has it sideways in his mouth now and he is moving off with it."

Then he will turn and swallow it, he thought. He did not say that because he knew that if you said a good thing it might not happen. He knew what a huge fish this was and he thought of him moving away in the darkness with the tuna held crosswise in his mouth. At that moment he felt him stop moving but the weight was still there. Then the weight increased and he gave more line. He tightened the pressure of his thumb and finger for a moment and the weight increased and was going straight down.

"He's taken it," he said. "Now I'll let him eat it well."

He let the line slip through his fingers while he reached down with his left hand and made fast the free end of the two reserve coils to the loop of the two reserve coils of the next line. Now he was ready. He had three forty-fathom coils of line in reserve now, as well as the coil he was using.

"Eat it a little more," he said. "Eat it well."

Eat it so that the point of the hook goes into your heart and kills you, he thought. Come up easy and let me put the harpoon into you. All right. Are you ready? Have you been long enough at table?

"Now!" he said aloud and struck hard with both hands, gained a yard of line and then struck again and again, swinging with each arm alternately on the cord with all the strength of his arms and the pivoted weight of his body.

Nothing happened. The fish just moved away slowly and the old man could not raise him an inch. His line was strong and made for heavy fish and he held it against his back until it was so taut that beads of water were jumping from it. Then

it began to make a slow hissing sound in the water and he still held it, bracing himself against the thwart and leaning back against the pull. The boat began to move slowly off toward the north-west.

The fish moved steadily and they travelled slowly on the calm water. The other baits were still in the water but there was nothing to be done.

"I wish I had the boy," the old man said aloud. "I'm being towed by a fish and I'm the towing bitt. I could make the line fast. But then he could break it. I must hold him all I can and give him line when he must have it. Thank God he is travelling and not going down."

What I will do if he decides to go down, I don't know. What I'll do if he sounds and dies I don't know. But I'll do something. There are plenty of things I can do.

He held the line against his back and watched its slant in the water and the skiff moving steadily to the north-west.

This will kill him, the old man thought. He can't do this forever. But four hours later the fish was still swimming steadily out to sea, towing the skiff, and the old man was still braced solidly with the line across his back.

"It was noon when I hooked him," he said. "And I have never seen him."

He had pushed his straw hat hard down on his head before he hooked the fish and it was cutting his forehead. He was thirsty too and he got down on his knees and, being careful not to jerk on the line, moved as far into the bow as he could get and reached the water bottle with one hand. He opened it and drank a little. Then he rested against the bow. He rested sitting on the un-stepped mast and sail and tried not to think but only to endure.

Then he looked behind him and saw that no land was visible. That makes no difference, he thought. I can always come in on the glow from Havana. There are two more hours before the sun sets and maybe he will come up before that. If he doesn't maybe he will come up with the moon. If he does not do that maybe he will come up with the sunrise. I have no cramps and I feel strong. It is he that has the hook in his mouth. But what a fish to pull like that. He must have his mouth shut tight on the wire. I wish I could see him. I wish I could see him only once to know what I have against me.

The fish never changed his course nor his direction all that night as far as the man could tell from watching the stars. It was cold after the sun went down and the old man's sweat dried cold on his back and his arms and his old legs. During the day he had taken the sack that covered the bait box and spread it in the sun to dry. After the sun went down he tied it around his neck so that it hung down over his back and he cautiously worked it down under the line that was across his shoulders now. The sack cushioned the line and he had found a way of leaning forward against the bow so that he was almost comfortable. The position actually was only somewhat less intolerable; but he thought of it as almost comfortable.

I can do nothing with him and he can do nothing with me, he thought. Not as long as he keeps this up.

Once he stood up and urinated over the side of the skiff and looked at the stars and checked his course. The line showed like a phosphorescent streak in the water straight out from his shoulders. They were moving more slowly now and the glow of Havana was not so strong, so that he knew the current must be carrying them to the eastward. If I lose the glare of Havana we must be going more to the eastward, he thought. For if the fish's course held true I must see it for many more hours. I wonder how the baseball came out in the grand leagues today, he thought. It would be wonderful to do this with a radio. Then he thought, think of it always. Think of what you are doing. You must do nothing stupid.

Then he said aloud, "I wish I had the boy. To help me and to see this."

No one should be alone in their old age, he thought. But it is unavoidable. I must remember to eat the tuna before he spoils in order to keep strong. Remember, no matter how little you want to, that you must eat him in the morning. Remember, he said to himself.

During the night two porpoises came around the boat and he could hear them rolling and blowing. He could tell the difference between the blowing noise the male made and the sighing blow of the female.

"They are good," he said. "They play and make jokes and love one another. They are our brothers like the flying fish."

Then he began to pity the great fish that he had hooked. He is wonderful and strange and who knows how old he is, he thought. Never have I had such a strong fish nor one who acted so strangely. Perhaps he is too wise to jump. He could ruin me by jumping or by a wild rush. But perhaps he has been hooked many times before and he knows that this is how he should make his fight. He cannot know that it is only one man against him, nor that it is an old man. But what a great fish he is and what will he bring in the market if the

flesh is good. He took the bait like a male and he pulls like a male and his fight has no panic in it. I wonder if he has any plans or if he is just as desperate as I am?

He remembered the time he had hooked one of a pair of marlin. The male fish always let the female fish feed first and the hooked fish, the female, made a wild, panic-stricken, despairing fight that soon exhausted her, and all the time the male had stayed with her, crossing the line and circling with her on the surface. He had stayed so close that the old man was afraid he would cut the line with his tail which was sharp as a scythe and almost of that size and shape. When the old man had gaffed her and clubbed her, holding the rapier bill with its sandpaper edge and clubbing her across the top of her head until her color turned to a color almost like the backing of mirrors, and then, with the boy's aid, hoisted her aboard, the male fish had stayed by the side of the boat. Then, while the old man was clearing the lines and preparing the harpoon, the male fish jumped high into the air beside the boat to see where the female was and then went down deep, his lavender wings, that were his pectoral fins, spread wide and all his wide lavender stripes showing. He was beautiful, the old man remembered, and he had stayed.

That was the saddest thing I ever saw with them, the old man thought. The boy was sad too and we begged her pardon and butchered her promptly.

"I wish the boy was here," he said aloud and settled himself against the rounded planks of the bow and felt the strength of the great fish through the line he held across his shoulders moving steadily toward whatever he had chosen.

When once, through my treachery, it had been necessary to him to make a choice, the old man thought.

His choice had been to stay in the deep dark water far out beyond all snares and traps and treacheries. My choice was to go there to find him beyond all people. Beyond all people in the world. Now we are joined together and have been since noon. And no one to help either one of us.

Perhaps I should not have been a fisherman, he thought. But that was the thing that I was born for. I must surely remember to eat the tuna after it gets light.

Some time before daylight something took one of the baits that were behind him. He heard the stick break and the line begin to rush out over the gunwale of the skiff. In the darkness he loosened his sheath knife and taking all the strain of the fish on his left shoulder he leaned back and cut the line against the wood of the gunwale. Then he cut the other line closest to him and in the dark made the loose ends of the reserve coils fast. He worked skillfully with the one hand and put his foot on the coils to hold them as he drew his knots tight. Now he had six reserve coils of line. There were two from each bait he had severed and the two from the bait the fish had taken and they were all connected.

After it is light, he thought, I will work back to the forty-fathom bait and cut it away too and link up the reserve coils.

I will have lost two hundred fathoms of good Catalan *cardel* and the hooks and leaders. That can be replaced. But who replaces this fish if I hook some fish and it cuts him off? I don't know what that fish was that took the bait just now. It could have been a marlin or a broadbill or a shark. I never felt him. I had to get rid of him too fast.

Aloud he said, "I wish I had the boy."

But you haven't got the boy, he thought. You have only yourself and you had better work back to the last line now, in the dark or not in the dark, and cut it away and hook up the two reserve coils.

So he did it. It was difficult in the dark and once the fish made a surge that pulled him down on his face and made a cut below his eye. The blood ran down his cheek a little way. But it coagulated and dried before it reached his chin and he worked his way back to the bow and rested against the wood. He adjusted the sack and carefully worked the line so that it came across a new part of his shoulders and, holding it anchored with his shoulders, he carefully felt the pull of the fish and then felt with his hand the progress of the skiff through the water.

I wonder what he made that lurch for, he thought. The wire must have slipped on the great hill of his back. Certainly his back cannot feel as badly as mine does. But he cannot pull this skiff forever, no matter how great he is. Now everything is cleared away that might make trouble and I have a big reserve of line; all that a man can ask.

"Fish," he said softly, aloud, "I'll stay with you until I am dead."

He'll stay with me too, I suppose, the old man thought and he waited for it to be light. It was cold now in the time before daylight and he pushed against the wood to be warm. I can do it as long as he can, he thought. And in the first light the line extended out and down into the water. The boat moved steadily and when the first edge of the sun rose it was on the old man's right shoulder.

"He's headed north," the old man said. The current will have set us far to the eastward, he thought. I wish he would turn with the current. That would show that he was tiring.

When the sun had risen further the old man realized that the fish was not tiring. There was only one favorable sign. The slant of the line showed he was swimming at a lesser depth. That did not necessarily mean that he would jump. But he might.

"God let him jump," the old man said. "I have enough line to handle him."

Maybe if I can increase the tension just a little it will hurt him and he will jump, he thought. Now that it is daylight let

him jump so that he'll fill the sacks along his backbone with air and then he cannot go deep to die.

He tried to increase the tension, but the line had been taut up to the very edge of the breaking point since he had hooked the fish and he felt the harshness as he leaned back to pull and knew he could put no more strain on it. I must not jerk it ever, he thought. Each jerk widens the cut the hook makes and then when he does jump he might throw it. Anyway I feel better with the sun and for once I do not have to look into it.

There was yellow weed on the line but the old man knew that only made an added drag and he was pleased. It was the yellow Gulf weed that had made so much phosphorescence in the night.

"Fish," he said, "I love you and respect you very much. But I will kill you dead before this day ends."

Let us hope so, he thought.

A small bird came toward the skiff from the north. He was a warbler and flying very low over the water. The old man could see that he was very tired.

The bird made the stern of the boat and rested there. Then he flew around the old man's head and rested on the line where he was more comfortable.

"How old are you?" the old man asked the bird. "Is this your first trip?"

The bird looked at him when he spoke. He was too tired even to examine the line and he teetered on it as his delicate feet gripped it fast.

"It's steady," the old man told him. "It's too steady. You shouldn't be that tired after a windless night. What are birds coming to?"

The hawks, he thought, that come out to sea to meet them. But he said nothing of this to the bird who could not understand him anyway and who would learn about the hawks soon enough.

"Take a good rest, small bird," he said. "Then go in and take your chance like any man or bird or fish."

It encouraged him to talk because his back had stiffened in the night and it hurt truly now.

"Stay at my house if you like, bird," he said. "I am sorry I cannot hoist the sail and take you in with the small breeze that is rising. But I am with a friend."

Just then the fish gave a sudden lurch that pulled the old man down onto the bow and would have pulled him overboard if he had not braced himself and given some line.

The bird had flown up when the line jerked and the old man had not even seen him go. He felt the line carefully with his right hand and noticed his hand was bleeding.

"Something hurt him then," he said aloud and pulled back on the line to see if he could turn the fish. But when he was touching the breaking point he held steady and settled back against the strain of the line.

"You're feeling it now, fish," he said. "And so, God knows, am I."

He looked around for the bird now because he would have liked him for company. The bird was gone.

You did not stay long, the man thought. But it is rougher where you are going until you make the shore. How did I let the fish cut me with that one quick pull he made? I must be getting very stupid. Or perhaps I was looking at the small bird and thinking of him. Now I will pay attention to my work and then I must eat the tuna so that I will not have a failure of strength.

"I wish the boy were here and that I had some salt," he said aloud.

Shifting the weight of the line to his left shoulder and kneeling carefully he washed his hand in the ocean and held it there, submerged, for more than a minute watching the blood trail away and the steady movement of the water against his hand as the boat moved.

"He has slowed much," he said.

The old man would have liked to keep his hand in the salt water longer but he was afraid of another sudden lurch by the fish and he stood up and braced himself and held his hand up against the sun. It was only a line burn that had cut

his flesh. But it was in the working part of his hand. He knew he would need his hands before this was over and he did not like to be cut before it started.

"Now," he said, when his hand had dried, "I must eat the small tuna. I can reach him with the gaff and eat him here in comfort."

He knelt down and found the tuna under the stern with the gaff and drew it toward him keeping it clear of the coiled lines. Holding the line with his left shoulder again, and bracing on his left hand and arm, he took the tuna off the gaff hook and put the gaff back in place. He put one knee on the fish and cut strips of dark red meat longitudinally from the back of the head to the tail. They were wedge-shaped strips and he cut them from next to the backbone down to the edge of the belly. When he had cut six strips he spread them out on the wood of the bow, wiped his knife on his trousers, and lifted the carcass of the bonito by the tail and dropped it overboard.

"I don't think I can eat an entire one," he said and drew his knife across one of the strips. He could feel the steady hard pull of the line and his left hand was cramped. It drew up tight on the heavy cord and he looked at it in disgust.

"What kind of a hand is that," he said. "Cramp then if you want. Make yourself into a claw. It will do you no good."

Come on, he thought and looked down into the dark water at the slant of the line. Eat it now and it will strengthen the hand. It is not the hand's fault and you have been many hours with the fish. But you can stay with him forever. Eat the bonito now.

He picked up a piece and put it in his mouth and chewed it slowly. It was not unpleasant.

Chew it well, he thought, and get all the juices. It would not be bad to eat with a little lime or with lemon or with salt.

"How do you feel, hand?" he asked the cramped hand that was almost as stiff as rigor mortis. "I'll eat some more for you."

He ate the other part of the piece that he had cut in two. He chewed it carefully and then spat out the skin.

"How does it go, hand? Or is it too early to know?"

He took another full piece and chewed it.

"It is a strong full-blooded fish," he thought. "I was lucky to get him instead of dolphin. Dolphin is too sweet. This is hardly sweet at all and all the strength is still in it."

There is no sense in being anything but practical though, he thought. I wish I had some salt. And I do not know whether the sun will rot or dry what is left, so I had better eat it all although I am not hungry. The fish is calm and steady. I will eat it all and then I will be ready.

"Be patient, hand," he said. "I do this for you."

I wish I could feed the fish, he thought. He is my brother. But I must kill him and keep strong to do it. Slowly and conscientiously he ate all of the wedge-shaped strips of fish.

He straightened up, wiping his hand on his trousers.

"Now," he said. "You can let the cord go, hand, and I will handle him with the right arm alone until you stop that nonsense." He put his left foot on the heavy line that the left hand had held and lay back against the pull against his back.

"God help me to have the cramp go," he said. "Because I do not know what the fish is going to do."

But he seems calm, he thought, and following his plan. But what is his plan, he thought. And what is mine? Mine I must improvise to his because of his great size. If he will jump I can kill him. But he stays down forever. Then I will stay down with him forever.

He rubbed the cramped hand against his trousers and tried to gentle the fingers. But it would not open. Maybe it will open with the sun, he thought. Maybe it will open when the strong raw tuna is digested. If I have to have it, I will open it, cost whatever it costs. But I do not want to open it now by force. Let it open by itself and come back of its own accord. After all I abused it much in the night when it was necessary to free and untie the various lines.

He looked across the sea and knew how alone he was now. But he could see the prisms in the deep dark water and the line stretching ahead and the strange undulation of the calm. The clouds were building up now for the trade wind and he looked ahead and saw a flight of wild ducks etching themselves against the sky over the water, then blurring, then etching again and he knew no man was ever alone on the sea.

He thought of how some men feared being out of sight of land in a small boat and knew they were right in the months of sudden bad weather. But now they were in hurricane months and, when there are no hurricanes, the weather of hurricane months is the best of all the year.

If there is a hurricane you always see the signs of it in the sky for days ahead, if you are at sea. They do not see it ashore because they do not know what to look for, he thought. The land must make a difference too, in the shape of the clouds. But we have no hurricane coming now.

He looked at the sky and saw the white cumulus built like friendly piles of ice cream and high above were the thin feathers of the cirrus against the high September sky.

"Light *brisa*[†]," he said. "Better weather for me than for you, fish."

His left hand was still cramped, but he was unknotting it slowly.

I hate a cramp, he thought. It is a treachery of one's own body. It is humiliating before others to have a diarrhea from ptomaine poisoning or to vomit from it. But a cramp, he thought of it as a *calambre*[†], humiliates oneself especially when one is alone.

If the boy were here he could rub it for me and loosen it down from the forearm, he thought. But it will loosen up.

Then, with his right hand he felt the difference in the pull of the line before he saw the slant change in the water. Then, as

[†] (Spanish) *brisa*: breeze
[†] (Spanish) *calambre*: a muscle cramp

he leaned against the line and slapped his left hand hard and fast against his thigh he saw the line slanting slowly upward.

"He's coming up," he said. "Come on hand. Please come on."

The line rose slowly and steadily and then the surface of the ocean bulged ahead of the boat and the fish came out. He came out unendingly and water poured from his sides. He was bright in the sun and his head and back were dark purple and in the sun the stripes on his sides showed wide and a light lavender. His sword was as long as a baseball bat and tapered like a rapier and he rose his full length from the water and then re-entered it, smoothly, like a diver and the old man saw the great scythe-blade of his tail go under and the line commenced to race out.

"He is two feet longer than the skiff," the old man said. The line was going out fast but steadily and the fish was not panicked. The old man was trying with both hands to keep the line just inside of breaking strength. He knew that if he could not slow the fish with a steady pressure the fish could take out all the line and break it.

He is a great fish and I must convince him, he thought. I must never let him learn his strength nor what he could do if he made his run. If I were him I would put in everything now and go until something broke. But, thank God, they are not as intelligent as we who kill them; although they are more noble and more able.

The old man had seen many great fish. He had seen many

that weighed more than a thousand pounds and he had caught two of that size in his life, but never alone. Now alone, and out of sight of land, he was fast to the biggest fish that he had ever seen and bigger than he had ever heard of, and his left hand was still as tight as the gripped claws of an eagle.

It will uncramp though, he thought. Surely it will uncramp to help my right hand. There are three things that are brothers: the fish and my two hands. It must uncramp. It is unworthy of it to be cramped. The fish had slowed again and was going at his usual pace.

I wonder why he jumped, the old man thought. He jumped almost as though to show me how big he was. I know now, anyway, he thought. I wish I could show him what sort of man I am. But then he would see the cramped hand. Let him think I am more man than I am and I will be so. I wish I was the fish, he thought, with everything he has against only my will and my intelligence.

He settled comfortably against the wood and took his suffering as it came and the fish swam steadily and the boat moved slowly through the dark water. There was a small sea rising with the wind coming up from the east and at noon the old man's left hand was uncramped.

"Bad news for you, fish," he said and shifted the line over the sacks that covered his shoulders.

He was comfortable but suffering, although he did not admit the suffering at all.

"I am not religious," he said. "But I will say ten Our Fathers and ten Hail Marys that I should catch this fish, and I promise to make a pilgrimage to the Virgin of Cobre if I catch him. That is a promise."

He commenced to say his prayers mechanically. Sometimes he would be so tired that he could not remember the prayer and then he would say them fast so that they would come automatically. Hail Marys are easier to say than Our Fathers, he thought.

"Hail Mary full of Grace the Lord is with thee. Blessed art thou among women and blessed is the fruit of thy womb, Jesus. Holy Mary, Mother of God, pray for us sinners now and at the hour of our death. Amen." Then he added, "Blessed Virgin, pray for the death of this fish. Wonderful though he is."

With his prayers said, and feeling much better, but suffering exactly as much, and perhaps a little more, he leaned against the wood of the bow and began, mechanically, to work the fingers of his left hand.

The sun was hot now although the breeze was rising gently.

"I had better re-bait that little line out over the stern," he said. "If the fish decides to stay another night I will need to eat again and the water is low in the bottle. I don't think I can get anything but a dolphin here. But if I eat him fresh enough he won't be bad. I wish a flying fish would come on board tonight. But I have no light to attract them. A flying fish is excellent to eat raw and I would not have to cut him up. I must save all my strength now. Christ, I did not know he was so big."

"I'll kill him though," he said. "In all his greatness and his glory."

Although it is unjust, he thought. But I will show him what a man can do and what a man endures.

"I told the boy I was a strange old man," he said. "Now is when I must prove it."

The thousand times that he had proved it meant nothing. Now he was proving it again. Each time was a new time and he never thought about the past when he was doing it.

I wish he'd sleep and I could sleep and dream about the lions, he thought. Why are the lions the main thing that is left? Don't think, old man, he said to himself. Rest gently now against the wood and think of nothing. He is working. Work as little as you can.

It was getting into the afternoon and the boat still moved

slowly and steadily. But there was an added drag now from the easterly breeze and the old man rode gently with the small sea and the hurt of the cord across his back came to him easily and smoothly.

Once in the afternoon the line started to rise again. But the fish only continued to swim at a slightly higher level. The sun was on the old man's left arm and shoulder and on his back. So he knew the fish had turned east of north.

Now that he had seen him once, he could picture the fish swimming in the water with his purple pectoral fins set wide as wings and the great erect tail slicing through the dark. I wonder how much he sees at that depth, the old man thought. His eye is huge and a horse, with much less eye, can see in the dark. Once I could see quite well in the dark. Not in the absolute dark. But almost as a cat sees.

The sun and his steady movement of his fingers had uncramped his left hand now completely and he began to shift more of the strain to it and he shrugged the muscles of his back to shift the hurt of the cord a little.

"If you're not tired, fish," he said aloud, "you must be very strange."

He felt very tired now and he knew the night would come soon and he tried to think of other things. He thought of the Big Leagues, to him they were the *Gran Ligas*†, and he knew that the Yankees of New York were playing the *Tigres*† of Detroit.

This is the second day now that I do not know the result of the *juegos*†, he thought. But I must have confidence and I must be worthy of the great DiMaggio who does all things perfectly even with the pain of the bone spur in his heel. What is a bone spur? he asked himself. *Un espuela de hueso*†. We do not have them. Can it be as painful as the spur of a fighting cock in one's heel? I do not think I could endure that or the loss of the eye and of both eyes and continue to fight as the fighting cocks do. Man is not much beside the great birds and beasts. Still I would rather be that beast down there in the darkness of the sea.

---

† (Spanish) *Gran Ligas:* the Major Leagues
† (Spanish) *Tigres:* reference to the Detroit Tigers
† (Spanish) *juegos:* games
† (Spanish) *un espuela de hueso:* a bone spur.

"Unless sharks come," he said aloud. "If sharks come, God pity him and me."

Do you believe the great DiMaggio would stay with a fish as long as I will stay with this one? he thought. I am sure he would and more since he is young and strong. Also his father was a fisherman. But would the bone spur hurt him too much?

"I do not know," he said aloud. "I never had a bone spur."

As the sun set he remembered, to give himself more confidence, the time in the tavern at Casablanca when he had played the hand game with the great negro from Cienfuegos who was the strongest man on the docks. They had gone one day and one night with their elbows on a chalk line on the table and their forearms straight up and their hands gripped tight. Each one was trying to force the other's hand down onto the table. There was much betting and people went in and out of the room under the kerosene lights and he had looked at the arm and hand of the negro and at the negro's face. They changed the referees every four hours after the first eight so that the referees could sleep. Blood came out from under the fingernails of both his and the negro's hands and they looked each other in the eye and at their hands and forearms and the bettors went in and out of the room and sat on high chairs against the wall and watched. The walls were painted bright blue and were of wood and the lamps threw their shadows against them. The negro's shadow was huge and it moved on the wall as the breeze moved the lamps.

The odds would change back and forth all night and they fed the negro rum and lighted cigarettes for him. Then the negro, after the rum, would try for a tremendous effort and once he had the old man, who was not an old man then but was Santiago *El Campeón*†, nearly three inches off balance. But the old man had raised his hand up to dead even again. He was sure then that he had the negro, who was a fine man and a great athlete, beaten. And at daylight when the bettors were asking that it be called a draw and the referee was shaking his head, he had unleashed his effort and forced the hand of the negro down and down until it rested on the wood. The match had started on a Sunday morning and ended on a Monday morning. Many of the bettors had asked for a draw because they had to go to work on the docks loading sacks of

† (Spanish) The Champion

sugar or at the Havana Coal Company. Otherwise everyone would have wanted it to go to a finish. But he had finished it anyway and before anyone had to go to work.

For a long time after that everyone had called him The Champion and there had been a return match in the spring. But not much money was bet and he had won it quite easily since he had broken the confidence of the negro from Cienfuegos in the first match. After that he had a few matches and then no more. He decided that he could beat anyone if he wanted to badly enough and he decided that it was bad for his right hand for fishing. He had tried a few practice matches with his left hand. But his left hand had always been a traitor and would not do what he called on it to do and he did not trust it.

The sun will bake it out well now, he thought. It should not cramp on me again unless it gets too cold in the night. I wonder what this night will bring.

An airplane passed overhead on its course to Miami and he watched its shadow scaring up the schools of flying fish.

"With so much flying fish there should be dolphin," he said, and leaned back on the line to see if it was possible to gain any on his fish. But he could not and it stayed at the hardness and water-drop shivering that preceded breaking. The boat moved ahead slowly and he watched the airplane until he could no longer see it.

It must be very strange in an airplane, he thought. I

wonder what the sea looks like from that height? They should be able to see the fish well if they do not fly too high. I would like to fly very slowly at two hundred fathoms high and see the fish from above. In the turtle boats I was in the cross-trees of the mast-head and even at that height I saw much. The dolphin look greener from there and you can see their stripes and their purple spots and you can see all of the school as they swim. Why is it that all the fast-moving fish of the dark current have purple backs and usually purple stripes or spots? The dolphin looks green of course because he is really golden. But when he comes to feed, truly hungry, purple stripes show on his sides as on a marlin. Can it be anger, or the greater speed he makes that brings them out?

Just before it was dark, as they passed a great island of Sargasso weed that heaved and swung in the light sea as though the ocean were making love with something under a yellow blanket, his small line was taken by a dolphin. He saw it first when it jumped in the air, true gold in the last of the sun and bending and flapping wildly in the air. It jumped again and again in the acrobatics of its fear and he worked his way back to the stern and crouching and holding the big line with his right hand and arm, he pulled the dolphin in with his left hand, stepping on the gained line each time with his bare left foot. When the fish was at the stem, plunging and cutting from side to side in desperation, the old man leaned over the stern and lifted the burnished gold fish with its purple spots over the stem. Its jaws were working convulsively in quick bites against the hook and it pounded the bottom of the skiff with its long flat body, its tail and its head until he clubbed it across the shining golden head until it shivered and was still.

The old man unhooked the fish, re-baited the line with another sardine and tossed it over. Then he worked his way slowly back to the bow. He washed his left hand and wiped it on his trousers. Then he shifted the heavy line from his right hand to his left and washed his right hand in the sea while he watched the sun go into the ocean and the slant of the big cord.

"He hasn't changed at all," he said. But watching the movement of the water against his hand he noted that it was perceptibly slower.

"I'll lash the two oars together across the stern and that will slow him in the night," he said. "He's good for the night and so am I."

It would be better to gut the dolphin a little later to save the blood in the meat, he thought. I can do that a little later and lash the oars to make a drag at the same time. I had better keep the fish quiet now and not disturb him too much at sunset. The setting of the sun is a difficult time for all fish.

He let his hand dry in the air then grasped the line with it and eased himself as much as he could and allowed himself to be pulled forward against the wood so that the boat took the strain as much, or more, than he did.

I'm learning how to do it, he thought. This part of it anyway. Then too, remember he hasn't eaten since he took the bait and he is huge and needs much food. I have eaten the whole bonito. Tomorrow I will eat the dolphin. He called it *dorado*†. Perhaps I should eat some of it when I clean it. It will be harder to eat than the bonito. But, then, nothing is easy.

"How do you feel, fish?" he asked aloud. "I feel good and my left hand is better and I have food for a night and a day. Pull the boat, fish."

He did not truly feel good because the pain from the cord across his back had almost passed pain and gone into a dullness that he mistrusted. But I have had worse things than that, he thought. My hand is only cut a little and the cramp is gone from the other. My legs are all right. Also now I have gained on him in the question of sustenance.

It was dark now as it becomes dark quickly after the sun sets in September. He lay against the worn wood of the bow and rested all that he could. The first stars were out. He did

† (Spanish) gilding; gilt

not know the name of Rigel but he saw it and knew soon they would all be out and he would have all his distant friends.

"The fish is my friend too," he said aloud. "I have never seen or heard of such a fish. But I must kill him. I am glad we do not have to try to kill the stars."

Imagine if each day a man must try to kill the moon, he thought. The moon runs away. But imagine if a man each day should have to try to kill the sun? We were born lucky, he thought.

Then he was sorry for the great fish that had nothing to eat and his determination to kill him never relaxed in his sorrow for him. How many people will he feed, he thought. But are they worthy to eat him? No, of course not. There is no one worthy of eating him from the manner of his behavior and his great dignity.

I do not understand these things, he thought. But it is good that we do not have to try to kill the sun or the moon or the stars. It is enough to live on the sea and kill our true brothers.

Now, he thought, I must think about the drag. It has its perils and its merits. I may lose so much line that I will lose him, if he makes his effort and the drag made by the oars is in place and the boat loses all her lightness. Her lightness prolongs both our suffering but it is my safety since he has great speed that he has never yet employed. No matter what passes I must gut the dolphin so he does not spoil and eat some of him to be strong.

Now I will rest an hour more and feel that he is solid and steady before I move back to the stern to do the work and make the decision. In the meantime I can see how he acts and if he shows any changes. The oars are a good trick; but it has reached the time to play for safety. He is much fish still and I saw that the hook was in the corner of his mouth and he has kept his mouth tight shut. The punishment of the hook is nothing. The punishment of hunger, and that he is against something that he does not comprehend, is everything. Rest now, old man, and let him work until your next duty comes.

He rested for what he believed to be two hours. The moon did not rise now until late and he had no way of judging the time. Nor was he really resting except comparatively. He was still bearing the pull of the fish across his shoulders but he placed his left hand on the gunwale of the bow and confided more and more of the resistance to the fish to the skiff itself.

How simple it would be if I could make the line fast, he thought. But with one small lurch he could break it. I must cushion the pull of the line with my body and at all times be ready to give line with both hands.

"But you have not slept yet, old man," he said aloud. "It is half a day and a night and now another day and you have not slept. You must devise a way so that you sleep a little if he is quiet and steady. If you do not sleep you might become unclear in the head."

I'm clear enough in the head, he thought. Too clear. I am

as clear as the stars that are my brothers. Still I must sleep. They sleep and the moon and the sun sleep and even the ocean sleeps sometimes on certain days when there is no current and a flat calm.

But remember to sleep, he thought. Make yourself do it and devise some simple and sure way about the lines. Now go back and prepare the dolphin. It is too dangerous to rig the oars as a drag if you must sleep.

I could go without sleeping, he told himself. But it would be too dangerous.

He started to work his way back to the stern on his hands and knees, being careful not to jerk against the fish. He may be half asleep himself, he thought. But I do not want him to rest. He must pull until he dies.

Back in the stern he turned so that his left hand held the strain of the line across his shoulders and drew his knife from its sheath with his right hand. The stars were bright now and he saw the dolphin clearly and he pushed the blade of his knife into his head and drew him out from under the stern. He put one of his feet on the fish and slit him quickly from the vent up to the tip of his lower jaw. Then he put his knife down and gutted him with his right hand, scooping him clean and pulling the gills clear. He felt the maw heavy and slippery in his hands and he slit it open. There were two flying fish inside. They were fresh and hard and he laid them side by side and dropped the guts and the gills over the stern.

They sank leaving a trail of phosphorescence in the water. The dolphin was cold and a leprous gray-white now in the starlight and the old man skinned one side of him while he held his right foot on the fish's head. Then he turned him over and skinned the other side and cut each side off from the head down to the tail.

He slid the carcass overboard and looked to see if there was any swirl in the water. But there was only the light of its slow descent. He turned then and placed the two flying fish inside the two fillets of fish and putting his knife back in its sheath, he worked his way slowly back to the bow. His back was bent with the weight of the line across it and he carried the fish in his right hand.

Back in the bow he laid the two fillets of fish out on the wood with the flying fish beside them. After that he settled the line across his shoulders in a new place and held it again with his left hand resting on the gunwale. Then he leaned over the side and washed the flying fish in the water, noting the speed of the water against his hand. His hand was phosphorescent from skinning the fish and he watched the flow of the water against it. The flow was less strong and as he rubbed the side of his hand against the planking of the skiff, particles of phosphorus floated off and drifted slowly astern.

"He is tiring or he is resting," the old man said. "Now let me get through the eating of this dolphin and get some rest and a little sleep."

Under the stars and with the night colder all the time he ate half of one of the dolphin fillets and one of the flying fish, gutted and with its head cut off.

"What an excellent fish dolphin is to eat cooked," he said. "And what a miserable fish raw. I will never go in a boat again without salt or limes."

If I had brains I would have splashed water on the bow all day and drying, it would have made salt, he thought. But then I did not hook the dolphin until almost sunset. Still it was a lack of preparation. But I have chewed it all well and I am not nauseated.

The sky was clouding over to the east and one after another the stars he knew were gone. It looked now as though he were moving into a great canyon of clouds and the wind had dropped.

"There will be bad weather in three or four days," he said. "But not tonight and not tomorrow. Rig now to get some sleep, old man, while the fish is calm and steady."

He held the line tight in his right hand and then pushed his thigh against his right hand as he leaned all his weight against the wood of the bow. Then he passed the line a little lower on his shoulders and braced his left hand on it.

My right hand can hold it as long as it is braced, he thought. If it relaxes in sleep my left hand will wake me as the line goes out. It is hard on the right hand. But he is used to punishment. Even if I sleep twenty minutes or a half an hour it is good. He lay forward cramping himself against the

line with all of his body, putting all his weight onto his right hand, and he was asleep.

He did not dream of the lions but instead of a vast school of porpoises that stretched for eight or ten miles and it was in the time of their mating and they would leap high into the air and return into the same hole they had made in the water when they leaped.

Then he dreamed that he was in the village on his bed and there was a norther and he was very cold and his right arm was asleep because his head had rested on it instead of a pillow.

After that he began to dream of the long yellow beach and he saw the first of the lions come down onto it in the early dark and then the other lions came and he rested his chin on the wood of the bows where the ship lay anchored with the evening off-shore breeze and he waited to see if there would be more lions and he was happy.

The moon had been up for a long time but he slept on and the fish pulled on steadily and the boat moved into the tunnel of clouds.

He woke with the jerk of his right fist coming up against his face and the line burning out through his right hand. He had no feeling of his left hand but he braked all he could with his right and the line rushed out. Finally his left hand found the line and he leaned back against the line and now it burned his back and his left hand, and his left hand was taking all the strain and cutting badly. He looked back at the coils of line and they were feeding smoothly. Just then the fish jumped making a great bursting of the ocean and then a heavy fall. Then he jumped again and again and the boat was going fast although line was still racing out and the old man was raising the strain to breaking point and raising it to breaking point again and again. He had been pulled down tight onto the bow and his face was in the cut slice of dolphin

and he could not move.

This is what we waited for, he thought. So now let us take it.

Make him pay for the line, he thought. Make him pay for it.

He could not see the fish's jumps but only heard the breaking of the ocean and the heavy splash as he fell. The speed of the line was cutting his hands badly but he had always known this would happen and he tried to keep the cutting across the calloused parts and not let the line slip into the palm nor cut the fingers.

If the boy was here he would wet the coils of line, he thought. Yes. If the boy were here. If the boy were here.

The line went out and out and out but it was slowing now and he was making the fish earn each inch of it. Now he got his head up from the wood and out of the slice of fish that his cheek had crushed. Then he was on his knees and then he rose slowly to his feet. He was ceding line but more slowly all the time. He worked back to where he could feel with his foot the coils of line that he could not see. There was plenty of line still and now the fish had to pull the friction of all that new line through the water.

Yes, he thought. And now he has jumped more than a dozen times and filled the sacks along his back with air and he cannot go down deep to die where I cannot bring him up. He will start circling soon and then I must work on him. I wonder what started him so suddenly? Could it have been hunger that made him desperate, or was he frightened by

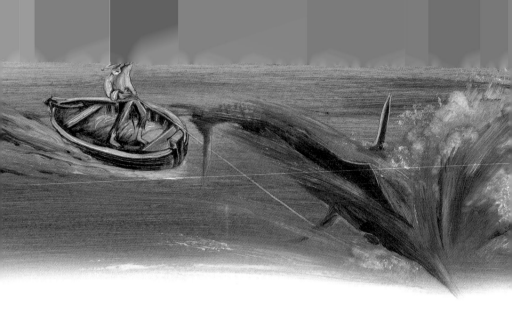

something in the night? Maybe he suddenly felt fear. But he was such a calm, strong fish and he seemed so fearless and so confident. It is strange.

"You better be fearless and confident yourself, old man," he said. "You're holding him again but you cannot get line. But soon he has to circle."

The old man held him with his left hand and his shoulders now and stooped down and scooped up water in his right hand to get the crushed dolphin flesh off of his face. He was afraid that it might nauseate him and he would vomit and lose his strength. When his face was cleaned he washed his right hand in the water over the side and then let it stay in the salt water while he watched the first light come before the sunrise. He's headed almost east, he thought. That means he is tired and going with the current. Soon he will have to circle. Then our true work begins.

After he judged that his right hand had been in the water

long enough he took it out and looked at it.

"It is not bad," he said. "And pain does not matter to a man."

He took hold of the line carefully so that it did not fit into any of the fresh line cuts and shifted his weight so that he could put his left hand into the sea on the other side of the skiff.

"You did not do so badly for something worthless," he said to his left hand. "But there was a moment when I could not find you."

Why was I not born with two good hands? he thought. Perhaps it was my fault in not training that one properly. But God knows he has had enough chances to learn. He did not do so badly in the night, though, and he has only cramped once. If he cramps again let the line cut him off.

When he thought that he knew that he was not being clear-headed and he thought he should chew some more of the dolphin. But I can't, he told himself. It is better to be light-headed than to lose your strength from nausea. And I know I cannot keep it if I eat it since my face was in it. I will keep it for an emergency until it goes bad. But it is too late to try for strength now through nourishment. You're stupid, he told himself. Eat the other flying fish.

It was there, cleaned and ready, and he picked it up with his left hand and ate it chewing the bones carefully and eating all of it down to the tail.

It has more nourishment than almost any fish, he thought. At least the kind of strength that I need. Now I have done what I can, he thought. Let him begin to circle and let the fight come.

The sun was rising for the third time since he had put to sea when the fish started to circle.

He could not see by the slant of the line that the fish was circling. It was too early for that. He just felt a faint slackening of the pressure of the line and he commenced to pull on it gently with his right hand. It tightened, as always, but just when he reached the point where it would break, line began to come in. He slipped his shoulders and head from under the line and began to pull in line steadily and gently. He used both of his hands in a swinging motion and tried to do the pulling as much as he could with his body and his legs. His old legs and shoulders pivoted with the swinging of the pulling.

"It is a very big circle," he said. "But he is circling."

Then the line would not come in any more and he held it until he saw the drops jumping from it in the sun. Then it started out and the old man knelt down and let it go grudgingly back into the dark water.

"He is making the far part of his circle now," he said. I must hold all I can, he thought. The strain will shorten his circle each time. Perhaps in an hour I will see him. Now I

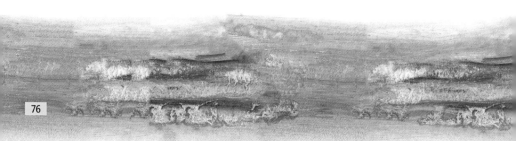

must convince him and then I must kill him.

But the fish kept on circling slowly and the old man was wet with sweat and tired deep into his bones two hours later. But the circles were much shorter now and from the way the line slanted he could tell the fish had risen steadily while he swam.

For an hour the old man had been seeing black spots before his eyes and the sweat salted his eyes and salted the cut over his eye and on his forehead. He was not afraid of the black spots. They were normal at the tension that he was pulling on the line. Twice, though, he had felt faint and dizzy and that had worried him.

"I could not fail myself and die on a fish like this," he said. "Now that I have him coming so beautifully, God help me endure. I'll say a hundred Our Fathers and a hundred Hail Marys. But I cannot say them now.

Consider them said, he thought. I'll say them later.

Just then he felt a sudden banging and jerking on the line he held with his two hands. It was sharp and hard-feeling and heavy.

He is hitting the wire leader with his spear, he thought. That was bound to come. He had to do that. It may make him jump though and I would rather he stayed circling now. The jumps were necessary for him to take air. But after that each one can widen the opening of the hook wound and he can throw the hook.

"Don't jump, fish," he said. "Don't jump."

The fish hit the wire several times more and each time he shook his head the old man gave up a little line.

I must hold his pain where it is, he thought. Mine does not matter. I can control mine. But his pain could drive him mad.

After a while the fish stopped beating at the wire and started circling slowly again. The old man was gaining line steadily now. But he felt faint again. He lifted some sea water with his left hand and put it on his head. Then he put more on and rubbed the back of his neck.

"I have no cramps," he said. "He'll be up soon and I can last. You have to last. Don't even speak of it."

He kneeled against the bow and, for a moment, slipped the line over his back again. I'll rest now while he goes out on the circle and then stand up and work on him when he comes in, he decided.

It was a great temptation to rest in the bow and let the fish make one circle by himself without recovering any line. But when the strain showed the fish had turned to come toward the boat, the old man rose to his feet and started the pivoting

and the weaving pulling that brought in all the line he gained.

I'm tireder than I have ever been, he thought, and now the trade wind is rising. But that will be good to take him in with. I need that badly.

"I'll rest on the next turn as he goes out," he said. "I feel much better. Then in two or three turns more I will have him."

His straw hat was far on the back of his head and he sank down into the bow with the pull of the line as he felt the fish turn.

You work now, fish, he thought. I'll take you at the turn.

The sea had risen considerably. But it was a fair-weather breeze and he had to have it to get home.

"I'll just steer south and west," he said. "A man is never lost at sea and it is a long island."

It was on the third turn that he saw the fish first.

He saw him first as a dark shadow that took so long to pass under the boat that he could not believe its length.

"No," he said. "He can't be that big."

But he was that big and at the end of this circle he came to the surface only thirty yards away and the man saw his tail out of water. It was higher than a big scythe blade and a very pale lavender above the dark blue water. It raked back and as the fish swam just below the surface the old man could see his huge bulk and the purple stripes that banded him. His dorsal fin was down and his huge pectorals were spread wide.

On this circle the old man could see the fish's eye and the two gray sucking fish that swam around him. Sometimes they attached themselves to him. Sometimes they darted off. Sometimes they would swim easily in his shadow. They were each over three feet long and when they swam fast they lashed their whole bodies like eels.

The old man was sweating now but from something else besides the sun. On each calm placid turn the fish made he was gaining line and he was sure that in two turns more he would have a chance to get the harpoon in.

But I must get him close, close, close, he thought. I mustn't try for the head. I must get the heart.

"Be calm and strong, old man," he said.

On the next circle the fish's back was out but he was a little too far from the boat. On the next circle he was still too far away but he was higher out of water and the old man was sure that by gaining some more line he could have him alongside.

He had rigged his harpoon long before and its coil of light rope was in a round basket and the end was made fast to the bitt in the bow.

The fish was coming in on his circle now calm and beautiful looking and only his great tail moving. The old man pulled on him all that he could to bring him closer. For just a moment the fish turned a little on his side. Then he straightened himself and began another circle.

"I moved him," the old man said. "I moved him then."

He felt faint again now but he held on the great fish all the strain that he could. I moved him, he thought. Maybe this time I can get him over. Pull, hands, he thought. Hold up, legs. Last for me, head. Last for me. You never went. This time I'll pull him over.

But when he put all of his effort on, starting it well out before the fish came alongside and pulling with all his strength, the fish pulled part way over and then righted himself and swam away.

"Fish," the old man said. "Fish, you are going to have to die anyway. Do you have to kill me too?"

That way nothing is accomplished, he thought. His mouth was too dry to speak but he could not reach for the water now. I must get him alongside this time, he thought. I am not good for many more turns. Yes you are, he told himself. You're good for ever.

On the next turn, he nearly had him. But again the fish righted himself and swam slowly away.

You are killing me, fish, the old man thought. But you have a right to. Never have I seen a greater, or more beautiful, or a calmer or more noble thing than you, brother. Come on and kill me. I do not care who kills who.

Now you are getting confused in the head, he thought. You must keep your head clear. Keep your head clear and know how to suffer like a man. Or a fish, he thought.

"Clear up, head," he said in a voice he could hardly hear. "Clear up."

Twice more it was the same on the turns.

I do not know, the old man thought. He had been on the point of feeling himself go each time. I do not know. But I will try it once more.

He tried it once more and he felt himself going when he turned the fish. The fish righted himself and swam off again slowly with the great tail weaving in the air.

I'll try it again, the old man promised, although his hands

were mushy now and he could only see well in flashes.

He tried it again and it was the same. So he thought, and he felt himself going before he started; I will try it once again.

He took all his pain and what was left of his strength and his long gone pride and he put it against the fish's agony and the fish came over onto his side and swam gently on his side, his bill almost touching the planking of the skiff and started to pass the boat, long, deep, wide, silver and barred with purple and interminable in the water.

The old man dropped the line and put his foot on it and lifted the harpoon as high as he could and drove it down with all his strength, and more strength he had just summoned, into the fish's side just behind the great chest fin that rose high in the air to the altitude of the man's chest. He felt the iron go in and he leaned on it and drove it further and then pushed all his weight after it.

Then the fish came alive, with his death in him, and rose high out of the water showing all his great length and width and all his power and his beauty. He seemed to hang in the air above the old man in the skiff. Then he fell into the water with a crash that sent spray over the old man and over all of the skiff.

The old man felt faint and sick and he could not see well. But he cleared the harpoon line and let it run slowly through his raw hands and, when he could see, he saw the fish was on his back with his silver belly up. The shaft of the harpoon was projecting at an angle from the fish's shoulder and the sea was discoloring with the red of the blood from his heart. First it was dark as a shoal in the blue water that was more than a mile deep. Then it spread like a cloud. The fish was silvery and still and floated with the waves.

The old man looked carefully in the glimpse of vision that he had. Then he took two turns of the harpoon line around the bitt in the bow and laid his head on his hands.

"Keep my head clear," he said against the wood of the bow. "I am a tired old man. But I have killed this fish which is my

brother and now I must do the slave work."

Now I must prepare the nooses and the rope to lash him alongside, he thought. Even if we were two and swamped her to load him and bailed her out, this skiff would never hold him. I must prepare everything, then bring him in and lash him well and step the mast and set sail for home.

He started to pull the fish in to have him alongside so that he could pass a line through his gills and out his mouth and make his head fast alongside the bow. I want to see him, he thought, and to touch and to feel him. He is my fortune, he thought. But that is not why I wish to feel him. I think I felt his heart, he thought. When I pushed on the harpoon shaft the second time. Bring him in now and make him fast and get the noose around his tail and another around his middle to bind him to the skiff.

"Get to work, old man," he said. He took a very small drink of the water. "There is very much slave work to be done now that the fight is over."

He looked up at the sky and then out to his fish. He looked

at the sun carefully. It is not much more than noon, he thought. And the trade wind is rising. The lines all mean nothing now. The boy and I will splice them when we are home.

"Come on, fish," he said. But the fish did not come. Instead he lay there wallowing now in the seas and the old man pulled the skiff up onto him.

When he was even with him and had the fish's head against the bow he could not believe his size. But he untied the harpoon rope from the bitt, passed it through the fish's gills and out his jaws, made a turn around his sword then passed the rope through the other gill, made another turn around the bill and knotted the double rope and made it fast to the bitt in the bow. He cut the rope then and went astern to noose the tail. The fish had turned silver from his original purple and silver, and the stripes showed the same pale violet color as his tail. They were wider than a man's hand with his fingers spread and the fish's eye looked as detached as the mirrors in a periscope or as a saint in a procession.

"It was the only way to kill him," the old man said. He was feeling better since the water and he knew he would not go away and his head was clear. He's over fifteen hundred pounds the way he is, he thought. Maybe much more. If he dresses out two-thirds of that at thirty cents a pound?

"I need a pencil for that," he said. "My head is not that clear. But I think the great DiMaggio would be proud of me today. I had no bone spurs. But the hands and the back hurt

truly." I wonder what a bone spur is, he thought. Maybe we have them without knowing of it.

He made the fish fast to bow and stern and to the middle thwart. He was so big it was like lashing a much bigger skiff alongside. He cut a piece of line and tied the fish's lower jaw against his bill so his mouth would not open and they would sail as cleanly as possible. Then he stepped the mast and, with the stick that was his gaff and with his boom rigged, the patched sail drew, the boat began to move, and half lying in the stern he sailed south-west.

He did not need a compass to tell him where southwest was. He only needed the feel of the trade wind and the drawing of the sail. I better put a small line out with a spoon on it and try and get something to eat and drink for the moisture. But he could not find a spoon and his sardines were rotten. So he hooked a patch of yellow Gulf weed with the gaff as they passed and shook it so that the small shrimps that were in it fell onto the planking of the skiff. There were more than a dozen of them and they jumped and kicked like sand fleas. The old man pinched their heads off with his thumb and forefinger and ate them chewing up the shells and the tails. They were very tiny but he knew they were nourishing and they tasted good.

The old man still had two drinks of water in the bottle and he used half of one after he had eaten the shrimps. The skiff was sailing well considering the handicaps and he steered with the tiller under his arm. He could see the fish and he had only to look at his hands and feel his back against the stern to know that this had truly happened and was not a dream. At one time when he was feeling so badly toward the end, he had thought perhaps it was a dream. Then when he had seen the fish come out of the water and hang motionless in the sky before he fell, he was sure there was some great strangeness and he could not believe it. Then he could not see well, although now he saw as well as ever.

Now he knew there was the fish and his hands and back were no dream. The hands cure quickly, he thought. I bled them clean and the salt water will heal them. The dark water of the true gulf is the greatest healer that there is. All I must do is keep the head clear. The hands have done their work and we sail well. With his mouth shut and his tail straight up and down we sail like brothers. Then his head started to become a little unclear and he thought, is he bringing me in or am I bringing him in? If I were towing him behind there would be no question. Nor if the fish were in the skiff, with

all dignity gone, there would be no question either. But they were sailing together lashed side by side and the old man thought, let him bring me in if it pleases him. I am only better than him through trickery and he meant me no harm.

They sailed well and the old man soaked his hands in the salt water and tried to keep his head clear. There were high cumulus clouds and enough cirrus above them so that the old man knew the breeze would last all night. The old man looked at the fish constantly to make sure it was true. It was an hour before the first shark hit him.

The shark was not an accident. He had come up from deep down in the water as the dark cloud of blood had settled and dispersed in the mile deep sea. He had come up so fast and absolutely without caution that he broke the surface of the blue water and was in the sun. Then he fell back into the sea and picked up the scent and started swimming on the course the skiff and the fish had taken.

Sometimes he lost the scent. But he would pick it up again, or have just a trace of it, and he swam fast and hard on the course. He was a very big Mako shark built to swim as fast as the fastest fish in the sea and everything about him was beautiful except his jaws. His back was as blue as a sword fish's and his belly was silver and his hide was smooth and handsome. He was built as a sword fish except for his huge jaws which were tight shut now as he swam fast, just under the surface with his high dorsal fin knifing through the water

without wavering. Inside the closed double lip of his jaws all of his eight rows of teeth were slanted inwards. They were not the ordinary pyramid-shaped teeth of most sharks. They were shaped like a man's fingers when they are crisped like claws. They were nearly as long as the fingers of the old man and they had razor-sharp cutting edges on both sides. This was a fish built to feed on all the fishes in the sea, that were so fast and strong and well armed that they had no other enemy. Now he speeded up as he smelled the fresher scent and his blue dorsal fin cut the water.

When the old man saw him coming he knew that this was a shark that had no fear at all and would do exactly what he wished. He prepared the harpoon and made the rope fast while he watched the shark come on. The rope was short as it lacked what he had cut away to lash the fish.

The old man's head was clear and good now and he was full of resolution but he had little hope. It was too good to last, he thought. He took one look at the great fish as he watched the shark close in. It might as well have been a dream, he thought. I cannot keep him from hitting me but maybe I can get him.

Dentuso†, he thought. Bad luck to your mother.

The shark closed fast astern and when he hit the fish the old man saw his mouth open and his strange eyes and the clicking chop of the teeth as he drove forward in the meat just above the tail. The shark's head was out of water and his back was coming out and the old man could hear the noise of skin and flesh ripping on the big fish when he rammed the harpoon down onto the shark's head at a spot where the line between his eyes intersected with the line that ran straight back from his nose. There were no such lines. There was only the heavy sharp blue head and the big eyes and the clicking, thrusting all-swallowing jaws. But that was the location of the brain and the old man hit it. He hit it with his blood mushed hands driving a good harpoon with all his strength. He hit it without hope but with resolution and complete malignancy.

The shark swung over and the old man saw his eye was not alive and then he swung over once again, wrapping

† (Spanish) big-toothed

himself in two loops of the rope. The old man knew that he was dead but the shark would not accept it. Then, on his back, with his tail lashing and his jaws clicking, the shark plowed over the water as a speedboat does. The water was white where his tail beat it and three-quarters of his body was clear above the water when the rope came taut, shivered, and then snapped. The shark lay quietly for a little while on the surface and the old man watched him. Then he went down very slowly.

"He took about forty pounds," the old man said aloud. He took my harpoon too and all the rope, he thought, and now my fish bleeds again and there will be others.

He did not like to look at the fish anymore since he had been mutilated. When the fish had been hit it was as though he himself were hit.

But I killed the shark that hit my fish, he thought. And he was the biggest *dentuso* that I have ever seen. And God knows that I have seen big ones.

It was too good to last, he thought. I wish it had been a dream now and that I had never hooked the fish and was alone in bed on the newspapers.

"But man is not made for defeat," he said. "A man can be destroyed but not defeated." I am sorry that I killed the fish though, he thought. Now the bad time is coming and I do not even have the harpoon. The *dentuso* is cruel and able and strong and intelligent. But I was more intelligent than he was. Perhaps not, he thought. Perhaps I was only better armed.

"Don't think, old man," he said aloud. "Sail on this course and take it when it comes."

But I must think, he thought. Because it is all I have left. That and baseball. I wonder how the great DiMaggio would have liked the way I hit him in the brain? It was no great thing, he thought. Any man could do it. But do you think my hands were as great a handicap as the bone spurs? I cannot know. I never had anything wrong with my heel except the time the sting ray stung it when I stepped on him when swimming and paralyzed the lower leg and made the unbearable pain.

"Think about something cheerful, old man," he said. "Every minute now you are closer to home. You sail lighter for the loss of forty pounds."

He knew quite well the pattern of what could happen when he reached the inner part of the current. But there was nothing to be done now.

"Yes there is," he said aloud. "I can lash my knife to the butt of one of the oars."

So he did that with the tiller under his arm and the sheet of the sail under his foot.

"Now," he said. "I am still an old man. But I am not unarmed."

The breeze was fresh now and he sailed on well. He watched only the forward part of the fish and some of his hope returned.

It is silly not to hope, he thought. Besides I believe it is a sin. Do not think about sin, he thought. There are enough problems now without sin. Also I have no understanding of it.

I have no understanding of it and I am not sure that I believe in it. Perhaps it was a sin to kill the fish. I suppose it was even though I did it to keep me alive and feed many people. But then everything is a sin. Do not think about sin. It is much too late for that and there are people who are paid to do it. Let them think about it. You were born to be a fisherman as the fish was born to be a fish. San Pedro was a fisherman as was the father of the great DiMaggio.

But he liked to think about all things that he was involved in and since there was nothing to read and he did not have a radio, he thought much and he kept on thinking about sin. You did not kill the fish only to keep alive and to sell for food, he thought. You killed him for pride and because you are a fisherman. You loved him when he was alive and you loved him

after. If you love him, it is not a sin to kill him. Or is it more?

"You think too much, old man," he said aloud.

But you enjoyed killing the *dentuso*, he thought. He lives on the live fish as you do. He is not a scavenger nor just a moving appetite as some sharks are. He is beautiful and noble and knows no fear of anything.

"I killed him in self-defense," the old man said aloud. "And I killed him well."

Besides, he thought, everything kills everything else in some way. Fishing kills me exactly as it keeps me alive. The boy keeps me alive, he thought. I must not deceive myself too much.

He leaned over the side and pulled loose a piece of the meat of the fish where the shark had cut him. He chewed it and noted its quality and its good taste. It was firm and juicy, like meat, but it was not red. There was no stringiness in it and he knew that it would bring the highest price in the market. But there was no way to keep its scent out of the water and the old man knew that a very bad time was coming.

The breeze was steady. It had backed a little further into the north-east and he knew that meant that it would not fall off. The old man looked ahead of him but he could see no sails nor could he see the hull nor the smoke of any ship. There were only the flying fish that went up from his bow sailing away to either side and the yellow patches of Gulf weed. He could not even see a bird.

He had sailed for two hours, resting in the stern and

sometimes chewing a bit of the meat from the marlin, trying to rest and to be strong, when he saw the first of the two sharks.

"*Ay*," he said aloud. There is no translation for this word and perhaps it is just a noise such as a man might make, involuntarily, feeling the nail go through his hands and into the wood.

"*Galanos*[†]," he said aloud. He had seen the second fin now coming up behind the first and had identified them as shovel-nosed sharks by the brown, triangular fin and the sweeping movements of the tail. They had the scent and were excited and in the stupidity of their great hunger they were losing and finding the scent in their excitement. But they were closing all the time.

The old man made the sheet fast and jammed the tiller. Then he took up the oar with the knife lashed to it. He lifted it as lightly as he could because his hands rebelled at the pain. Then he opened and closed them on it lightly to loosen them. He closed them firmly so they would take the pain now and would not flinch and watched the sharks come. He could see their wide, flattened, shovel-pointed heads now and their

white-tipped wide pectoral fins. They were hateful sharks, bad smelling, scavengers as well as killers, and when they were hungry they would bite at an oar or the rudder of a boat. It was these sharks that would cut the turtles' legs and flippers off when the turtles were asleep on the surface, and they would hit a man in the water, if they were hungry, even if the man had no smell of fish blood nor of fish slime on him.

"Ay," the old man said. "*Galanos*. Come on *galanos*."

They came. But they did not come as the Mako had come. One turned and went out of sight under the skiff and the old man could feel the skiff shake as he jerked and pulled on the fish. The other watched the old man with his slitted yellow eyes and then came in fast with his half circle of jaws wide to hit the fish where he had already been bitten. The line showed clearly on the top of his brown head and back where the brain joined the spinal cord and the old man drove the knife on the oar into the juncture, withdrew it, and drove it in again into the shark's yellow cat-like eyes. The shark let go of the fish and slid down, swallowing what he had taken as he died.

† (Spanish) mottled ones

The skiff was still shaking with the destruction the other shark was doing to the fish and the old man let go the sheet so that the skiff would swing broadside and bring the shark out from under. When he saw the shark he leaned over the side and punched at him. He hit only meat and the hide was set hard and he barely got the knife in. The blow hurt not only his hands but his shoulder too. But the shark came up fast with his head out and the old man hit him squarely in the center of his flat-topped head as his nose came out of water and lay against the fish. The old man withdrew the blade and punched the shark exactly in the same spot again. He still hung to the fish with his jaws hooked and the old man stabbed him in his left eye. The shark still hung there.

"No?" the old man said and he drove the blade between the vertebrae and the brain. It was an easy shot now and he felt the cartilage sever. The old man reversed the oar and put the blade between the shark's jaws to open them. He twisted the blade and as the shark slid loose he said, "Go on, *galano*. Slide down a mile deep. Go see your friend, or maybe it's your mother."

The old man wiped the blade of his knife and laid down the oar. Then he found the sheet and the sail filled and he brought the skiff onto her course.

"They must have taken a quarter of him and of the best meat," he said aloud. "I wish it were a dream and that I had never hooked him. I'm sorry about it, fish. It makes everything wrong." He stopped and he did not want to look at the fish

now. Drained of blood and awash he looked the color of the silver backing of a mirror and his stripes still showed.

"I shouldn't have gone out so far, fish," he said. "Neither for you nor for me. I'm sorry, fish."

Now, he said to himself. Look to the lashing on the knife and see if it has been cut. Then get your hand in order because there still is more to come.

"I wish I had a stone for the knife," the old man said after he had checked the lashing on the oar butt. "I should have brought a stone." You should have brought many things, he thought. But you did not bring them, old man. Now is no time to think of what you do not have. Think of what you can do with what there is.

"You give me much good counsel," he said aloud. "I'm tired of it."

He held the tiller under his arm and soaked both his hands in the water as the skiff drove forward.

"God knows how much that last one took," he said. "But she's much lighter now." He did not want to think of the mutilated under-side of the fish. He knew that each of the jerking bumps of the shark had been meat torn away and that the fish now made a trail for all sharks as wide as a highway through the sea.

He was a fish to keep a man all winter, he thought. Don't think of that. Just rest and try to get your hands in shape to defend what is left of him. The blood smell from my hands means nothing now with all that scent in the water. Besides they do not bleed much. There is nothing cut that means anything. The bleeding may keep the left from cramping.

What can I think of now? he thought. Nothing. I must think of nothing and wait for the next ones. I wish it had really been a dream, he thought. But who knows? It might have turned out well.

The next shark that came was a single shovelnose. He came like a pig to the trough if a pig had a mouth so wide that you could put your head in it. The old man let him hit the fish and then drove the knife on the oar down into his brain. But the shark jerked backwards as he rolled and the knife blade snapped.

The old man settled himself to steer. He did not even watch the big shark sinking slowly in the water, showing first life-size, then small, then tiny. That always fascinated the old man. But he did not even watch it now.

"I have the gaff now," he said. "But it will do no good. I have the two oars and the tiller and the short club."

Now they have beaten me, he thought. I am too old to club sharks to death. But I will try it as long as I have the oars and the short club and the tiller.

He put his hands in the water again to soak them. It was getting late in the afternoon and he saw nothing but the sea and the sky. There was more wind in the sky than there had been, and soon he hoped that he would see land.

"You're tired, old man," he said. "You're tired inside."

The sharks did not hit him again until just before sunset.

The old man saw the brown fins coming along the wide trail the fish must make in the water. They were not even quartering on the scent. They were headed straight for the skiff swimming side by side.

He jammed the tiller, made the sheet fast and reached under the stern for the club. It was an oar handle from a broken oar sawed off to about two and a half feet in length. He could only use it effectively with one hand because of the grip of the handle and he took good hold of it with his right hand, flexing his hand on it, as he watched the sharks come. They were both *galanos*.

I must let the first one get a good hold and hit him on the point of the nose or straight across the top of the head, he thought.

The two sharks closed together and as he saw the one nearest him open his jaws and sink them into the silver side of the fish, he raised the club high and brought it down heavy and slamming onto the top of the shark's broad head. He felt the rubbery solidity as the club came down. But he felt the rigidity of bone too and he struck the shark once more hard across the point of the nose as he slid down from the fish.

The other shark had been in and out and now came in again with his jaws wide. The old man could see pieces of the meat of the fish spilling white from the corner of his jaws as he bumped the fish and closed his jaws. He swung at him and hit only the head and the shark looked at him and wrenched the meat loose. The old man swung the club down on him again as he slipped away to swallow and hit only the heavy solid rubberiness.

"Come on, *galano*," the old man said. "Come in again."

The shark came in a rush and the old man hit him as he shut his jaws. He hit him solidly and from as high up as he could raise the club. This time he felt the bone at the base of the brain and he hit him again in the same place while the shark tore the meat loose sluggishly and slid down from the fish.

The old man watched for him to come again but neither shark showed. Then he saw one on the surface swimming in circles. He did not see the fin of the other.

I could not expect to kill them, he thought. I could have in my time. But I have hurt them both badly and neither one can feel very good. If I could have used a bat with two hands I could have killed the first one surely. Even now, he thought.

He did not want to look at the fish. He knew that half of him had been destroyed. The sun had gone down while he had been in the fight with the sharks.

"It will be dark soon," he said. "Then I should see the glow of Havana. If I am too far to the eastward I will see the lights of one of the new beaches."

I cannot be too far out now, he thought. I hope no one has been too worried. There is only the boy to worry, of course. But I am sure he would have confidence. Many of the older fishermen will worry. Many others too, he thought. I live in a good town.

He could not talk to the fish anymore because the fish had been ruined too badly. Then something came into his head.

"Half fish," he said. "Fish that you were. I am sorry that I went too far out. I ruined us both. But we have killed many sharks, you and I, and ruined many others. How many did you ever kill, old fish? You do not have that spear on your head for nothing."

He liked to think of the fish and what he could do to a shark if he were swimming free. I should have chopped the bill off to fight them with, he thought. But there was no hatchet and then there was no knife.

But if I had, and could have lashed it to an oar butt, what a weapon. Then we might have fought them together. What will you do now if they come in the night? What can you do?

"Fight them," he said. "I'll fight them until I die."

But in the dark now and no glow showing and no lights and only the wind and the steady pull of the sail he felt that perhaps he was already dead. He put his two hands together and felt the palms. They were not dead and he could bring the pain of life by simply opening and closing them. He leaned his back against the stern and knew he was not dead. His shoulders told him.

I have all those prayers I promised if I caught the fish, he thought. But I am too tired to say them now. I better get the sack and put it over my shoulders.

He lay in the stern and steered and watched for the glow to come in the sky. I have half of him, he thought. Maybe I'll have the luck to bring the forward half in. I should have some luck. No, he said. You violated your luck when you went too far outside.

"Don't be silly," he said aloud. "And keep awake and steer. You may have much luck yet."

"I'd like to buy some if there's any place they sell it," he said.

What could I buy it with? he asked himself. Could I buy it with a lost harpoon and a broken knife and two bad hands?

"You might," he said. "You tried to buy it with eighty-four days at sea. They nearly sold it to you too."

I must not think nonsense, he thought. Luck is a thing that comes in many forms and who can recognize her? I would take some though in any form and pay what they asked. I

wish I could see the glow from the lights, he thought. I wish too many things. But that is the thing I wish for now. He tried to settle more comfortably to steer and from his pain he knew he was not dead.

He saw the reflected glare of the lights of the city at what must have been around ten o'clock at night. They were only perceptible at first as the light is in the sky before the moon rises. Then they were steady to see across the ocean which was rough now with the increasing breeze. He steered inside of the glow and he thought that now, soon, he must hit the edge of the stream.

Now it is over, he thought. They will probably hit me again. But what can a man do against them in the dark without a weapon?

He was stiff and sore now and his wounds and all of the strained parts of his body hurt with the cold of the night. I hope I do not have to fight again, he thought. I hope so much I do not have to fight again.

But by midnight he fought and this time he knew the fight was useless. They came in a pack and he could only see the lines in the water that their fins made and their phosphorescence as they threw themselves on the fish. He clubbed at heads and heard the jaws chop and the shaking of the skiff as they took hold below. He clubbed desperately at what he could only feel and hear and he felt something seize the club and it was gone.

He jerked the tiller free from the rudder and beat and chopped with it, holding it in both hands and driving it down again and again. But they were up to the bow now and driving in one after the other and together, tearing off the pieces of meat that showed glowing below the sea as they turned to come once more.

One came, finally, against the head itself and he knew that it was over. He swung the tiller across the shark's head where the jaws were caught in the heaviness of the fish's head which would not tear. He swung it once and twice and again. He

heard the tiller break and he lunged at the shark with the splintered butt. He felt it go in and knowing it was sharp he drove it in again. The shark let go and rolled away. That was the last shark of the pack that came. There was nothing more for them to eat.

The old man could hardly breathe now and he felt a strange taste in his mouth. It was coppery and sweet and he was afraid of it for a moment. But there was not much of it.

He spat into the ocean and said, "Eat that, *galanos*. And make a dream you've killed a man."

He knew he was beaten now finally and without remedy and he went back to the stern and found the jagged end of the tiller would fit in the slot of the rudder well enough for him to steer. He settled the sack around his shoulders and put the skiff on her course. He sailed lightly now and he had no thoughts nor any feelings of any kind. He was past everything now and he sailed the skiff to make his home port as well and as intelligently as he could. In the night sharks hit the carcass as someone might pick up crumbs from the table. The old man paid no attention to them and did not pay any attention to anything except steering. He only noticed how lightly and how well the skiff sailed now there was no great weight beside her.

She's good, he thought. She is sound and not harmed in any way except for the tiller. That is easily replaced.

He could feel he was inside the current now and he could

see the lights of the beach colonies along the shore. He knew where he was now and it was nothing to get home.

The wind is our friend, anyway, he thought. Then he added, sometimes. And the great sea with our friends and our enemies. And bed, he thought. Bed is my friend. Just bed, he thought. Bed will be a great thing. It is easy when you are beaten, he thought. I never knew how easy it was. And what beat you, he thought.

"Nothing," he said aloud. "I went out too far."

When he sailed into the little harbor the lights of the Terrace were out and he knew everyone was in bed. The breeze had risen steadily and was blowing strongly now. It was quiet in the harbor though and he sailed up onto the little patch of shingle below the rocks. There was no one to help him so he pulled the boat up as far as he could. Then he stepped out and made her fast to a rock.

He unstepped the mast and furled the sail and tied it. Then he shouldered the mast and started to climb. It was then he knew the depth of his tiredness. He stopped for a moment and looked back and saw in the reflection from the street light the great tail of the fish standing up well behind the skiff's stern. He saw the white naked line of his backbone and the dark mass of the head with the projecting bill and all the nakedness between.

He started to climb again and at the top he fell and lay for some time with the mast across his shoulder. He tried to get up. But it was too difficult and he sat there with the mast on his shoulder and looked at the road. A cat passed on the far side going about its business and the old man watched it. Then he just watched the road.

Finally he put the mast down and stood up. He picked the mast up and put it on his shoulder and started up the road. He had to sit down five times before he reached his shack.

Inside the shack he leaned the mast against the wall. In the dark he found a water bottle and took a drink. Then he lay down on the bed. He pulled the blanket over his shoulders and then over his back and legs and he slept face down on the newspapers with his arms out straight and the palms of his hands up.

He was asleep when the boy looked in the door in the morning. It was blowing so hard that the drifting boats would not be going out and the boy had slept late and then come to the old man's shack as he had come each morning. The boy saw that the old man was breathing and then he saw the old man's hands and he started to cry. He went out very quietly to go to bring some coffee and all the way down the road he was crying.

Many fishermen were around the skiff looking at what was lashed beside it and one was in the water, his trousers rolled up, measuring the skeleton with a length of line.

The boy did not go down. He had been there before and one of the fishermen was looking after the skiff for him.

"How is he?" one of the fishermen shouted.

"Sleeping," the boy called. He did not care that they saw him crying. "Let no one disturb him."

"He was eighteen feet from nose to tail," the fisherman who was measuring him called.

"I believe it," the boy said.

He went into the Terrace and asked for a can of coffee.

"Hot and with plenty of milk and sugar in it."

"Anything more?"

"No. Afterwards I will see what he can eat."

"What a fish it was," the proprietor said. "There has never been such a fish. Those were two fine fish you took yesterday too."

"Damn my fish," the boy said and he started to cry again.

"Do you want a drink of any kind?" the proprietor asked.

"No," the boy said. "Tell them not to bother Santiago. I'll be back."

"Tell him how sorry I am."

"Thanks," the boy said.

The boy carried the hot can of coffee up to the old man's shack and sat by him until he woke. Once it looked as though he were waking. But he had gone back into heavy sleep and the boy had gone across the road to borrow some wood to heat the coffee.

Finally the old man woke.

"Don't sit up," the boy said. "Drink this." He poured some of the coffee in a glass.

The old man took it and drank it.

"They beat me, Manolin," he said. "They truly beat me."

"He didn't beat you. Not the fish."

"No. Truly. It was afterwards."

"Pedrico is looking after the skiff and the gear. What do you want done with the head?"

"Let Pedrico chop it up to use in fish traps."

"And the spear?"

"You keep it if you want it."

"I want it," the boy said. "Now we must make our plans about the other things."

"Did they search for me?"

"Of course. With coast guard and with planes."

"The ocean is very big and a skiff is small and hard to see," the old man said. He noticed how pleasant it was to have someone to talk to instead of speaking only to himself and to the sea. "I missed you," he said. "What did you catch?"

"One the first day. One the second and two the third."

"Very good."

"Now we fish together again."

"No. I am not lucky. I am not lucky anymore."

"The hell with luck," the boy said. "I'll bring the luck with me."

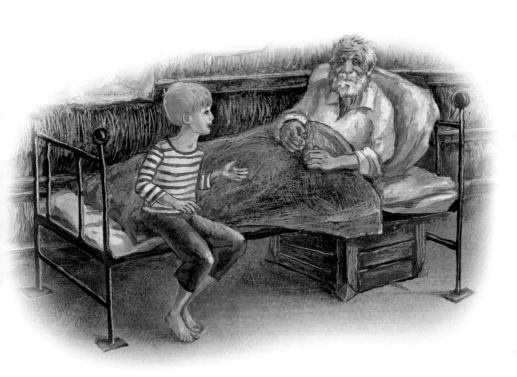

"What will your family say?"

"I do not care. I caught two yesterday. But we will fish together now for I still have much to learn."

"We must get a good killing lance and always have it on board. You can make the blade from a spring leaf from an old Ford. We can grind it in Guanabacoa. It should be sharp and not tempered so it will break. My knife broke."

"I'll get another knife and have the spring ground." How many days of heavy *brisa* have we?"

"Maybe three. Maybe more."

"I will have everything in order," the boy said. "You get your hands well old man."

"I know how to care for them. In the night I spat

something strange and felt something in my chest was broken."

"Get that well too," the boy said. "Lie down, old man, and I will bring you your clean shirt. And something to eat."

"Bring any of the papers of the time that I was gone," the old man said.

"You must get well fast for there is much that I can learn and you can teach me everything. How much did you suffer?"

"Plenty," the old man said.

"I'll bring the food and the papers," the boy said. "Rest well, old man. I will bring stuff from the drugstore for your hands."

"Don't forget to tell Pedrico the head is his."

"No. I will remember."

As the boy went out the door and down the worn coral rock road he was crying again.

That afternoon there was a party of tourists at the Terrace and looking down in the water among the empty beer cans and dead barracudas a woman saw a great long white spine with a huge tail at the end that lifted and swung with the tide while the east wind blew a heavy steady sea outside the entrance to the harbor.

"What's that?" she asked a waiter and pointed to the long backbone of the great fish that was now just garbage waiting to go out with the tide.

"Tiburon[†]," the waiter said. "Eshark." He was meaning to explain what had happened.

"I didn't know sharks had such handsome, beautifully formed tails."

"I didn't either," her male companion said.

Up the road, in his shack, the old man was sleeping again. He was still sleeping on his face and the boy was sitting by him watching him. The old man was dreaming about the lions.

† (Spanish) shark

老人與海

老人孤獨地划著一艘小船，在墨西哥灣航行了八十四天，卻連一條魚都沒有捕到。起初的四十天裡，還有一個小男孩跟著他，但四十天之後，由於沒有捕到魚，小男孩的父母便跟男孩說，這個老頭現在走衰運†，運氣背到極點了。小男孩只得聽從父母的命令，換跟別的船，而他們第一個星期就捕到了三條大魚。小孩每天看到老人一無所獲，駕著空船回來，心裡很難過。所以他都會跑去幫他拿線繩、魚鉤或魚叉等魚具，還有捲在桅杆上的船帆。帆面上補滿了麵粉袋的補釘，皺皺地捲在一起，看起來就像是一面永遠在吃敗仗的旗子。

老人瘦骨如柴又憔悴，頸部背後佈滿了深深的皺紋。陽光照射在熱帶海洋上，反射到老人的面頰，讓他從兩頰一直到雙手都長出了一塊塊的褐色斑點，這是良性的皮膚

† 此為西班牙語salao。原著中偶而會出現西班牙語，
　原著以斜體表示，中譯則以楷體表示。

瘤。他的雙手因為長期操作粗重的繩索，烙下了深深的勒痕。這些疤痕沒有一處是新的傷口，而是像無魚沙漠被侵蝕的痕跡。

他垂垂老矣，但一雙藍如大海的眼睛神采奕奕，好像從沒吃過敗仗似的。

　　「山帝亞哥。」他們爬上小船拖曳上岸的地方，小男孩叫著他的名字，說道：「我可以再和你一起捕魚，我們也賺過一些錢！」

　　老人教小男孩如何捕魚，小男孩很敬愛他。

　　「不，你現在跟的船正走運，你要繼續跟。」老人道。

　　「可是你記不記得，你有一次連續八十七天一條魚也沒捕到，後來接連三個星期每天都捕到大魚。」

　　「記得。」老人說：「我知道你不是因為對我沒信心才離開的。」

　　「是我爸叫我離開的。我還小，只得聽他的話。」

老人說：「我知道，這是理所當然的。」

　　「他沒什麼信心。」

　　「他是沒什麼信心，但我們有信心，對吧？」

　　「對！」小男孩說：「我請你到露天酒店喝杯啤酒，然後再把東西搬回家去。」

　　「好啊！」老人說：「反正大家都是打漁的。」

　　他們坐在露天酒店，很多漁夫嘲笑老人，但老人一點也不生氣。有些年紀較長的漁夫看著他，替他感到難過，可是並沒有很明顯地表露出來，他們禮貌性地聊著洋流、魚線要垂釣的深度、穩定的好天氣，以及海上的所見所聞。

當天滿載而歸的漁夫已經走了進來。他們把旗魚剖腹處理後，放在兩塊厚厚的木板上，一人抬著一頭，蹣跚地抬到魚庫裡，準備裝上冷凍車，運送到哈瓦那市場。而那些捕到鯊魚的漁夫們，則把鯊魚運往小海灣另一頭的鯊魚工廠，用滑輪把鯊魚垂吊起來，然後取下肝臟，割掉鰭，剝下皮，再把魚肉割成條狀，準備用鹽醃製。

　　只要吹起東風，鯊魚工廠的魚腥味便會從海灣對岸飄過來。但今天，露天酒店裡只嗅到微微的魚腥味，因為風往北方回吹而逝，酒店這邊風和日麗，陽光普照。

「山帝亞哥。」小男孩叫道。

「什麼事？」老人應了一聲。他的手握著杯子，回憶起多年前的往事。

「我可以去幫你準備明天要用的沙丁魚嗎？」

「不用了，你去打棒球吧！我還可以自己划船，而且羅吉里歐會幫忙撒網。」

「我想跟著去。雖然我不能跟船捕魚，但至少可以幫忙做些什麼。」

「你請我喝啤酒，你已經是個大人了。」老人說。

「你第一次帶我上船時，我幾歲？」

「五歲。你記不記得，那時我釣了一條很大的魚，因為太早把魚拖上來，船差一點四分五裂，要了你的小命。」

「我記得魚拍打著尾巴，撞斷了船板，還有你用棍棒敲打魚的聲音。我還記得你把我放在船頭，船頭有一些濕掉的繩索，那時我感覺整艘船都在搖晃，而你用棍子打魚的聲音，就像砍樹一樣那麼大聲，接著我全身上下都是新鮮的魚腥味。」

「你是真的記得這件事，還是因為我告訴你，你才想起來的？」

「我們第一次一起出海後的每件事我都記得很清楚。」

老人抬起被太陽曬黑的臉，用充滿信心和關愛的眼神望著小男孩。

「如果你是我的小孩，我一定帶你去碰碰運氣。可是你是別人家的孩子，而且你現在跟的船又很走運。」他說。

「我去弄點沙丁魚來好嗎？而且我知道可以去哪裡弄到四個魚餌。」

「沙丁魚我今天還剩一些，我已經把牠們放在盒子裡用鹽醃起來了。」

「我還是去弄四個新鮮的來好了。」

「一個就夠了。」老人說。他從不曾失去希望和信心，但在此刻吹起的微風中，希望和信心顯得蓄勢待發。

「兩個好了。」小男孩說。

「好吧！兩個就兩個。」老人同意，「你該不會用偷的吧？」

「有可能！」小男孩說：「不過這兩個我會用買的。」

「謝謝你。」老人說。他這個人很簡單，簡單到沒想過自己何時也變得謙虛了。但他知道自己是變謙虛了沒錯，而且不認為這有什麼好丟臉的，並不會損及自尊。

「從這樣的潮汐看來，明天是出船的好日子。」他說。

小男孩問：「你明天要去什麼地方？」

「我想出遠船，等風轉向時再折返。我想在天亮前就出發。」

「那我也要叫他把船開遠一點，這樣如果你釣到大魚，我們就可以過去幫你的忙。」小男孩說。

「他不喜歡出船太遠。」

小男孩說：「雖然他不喜歡，但我可以看見他看不到的東西，比如說鳥在叼魚時，我會叫他跟在鱰鰍[†]去後面捕魚。」

「他的視力這麼差嗎？」

「幾乎快瞎了。」

「那很奇怪，他又不捕龜，捕龜才會傷眼睛。」老人說。

「可是你在蚊子海岸捕龜那麼多年，視力還是很好。」

---

† 鱰鰍（dolphinfish），英文原著中以dolphin表示。

「我是一個奇怪的老頭子。」

「那你現在還有沒有體力捕超級大魚？」

「應該沒問題，而且我還有很多捕魚的訣竅。」

「我們先把這些東西搬回家，」小男孩說：「我好去拿網，然後再去找一些沙丁魚來。」

他們把船上的工具搬出來，老人把桅杆扛在肩上，小男孩拿著木箱，木箱裡裝滿數捲結實的棕色繩索，還有魚鉤和帶柄的魚叉。裝魚餌的箱子放在船尾，和棍棒放在一起，當大魚被拖到岸邊時，就用棍棒來制服。雖然沒有人會偷老人的東西，但把帆和魚線帶回家還是比較妥當，因為會被清晨的露水給浸濕。老人很確定當地人不會偷他的東西，但他認為不需要把魚鉤和魚叉留在船上引誘別人。

他們沿著路一起來到老人的小屋，走進大門敞開的屋子裡。老人把捲著帆的桅杆靠在牆上，小男孩把箱子和其他漁具放在桅杆旁，桅杆的長度幾乎快和小屋的房間一樣高。這間小屋用一種叫官糯王棕的堅韌葉梢所搭造，屋子

裡有一張床、一張桌子和一把椅子，泥地上有個空地可以燒煤炭煮飯。棕色的牆由纖維強韌官糯王棕葉所壓平重疊所蓋成，牆上掛了一幅彩色的耶穌聖心像，還有仁愛聖母†圖，這些是他妻子留下來的遺物。牆上原本還有一張妻子褪色的照片，但因為會觸景傷情，現在已經取下來，放在牆角的架子上，壓在乾淨的襯衫下面。

「你有什麼東西可以吃的？」小男孩問。

「一鍋黃米飯和魚，你要來一點嗎？」

「不用了，我要回家吃飯。要我生火嗎？」

「不必了，我待會再自己生火，或者我吃冷飯就好。」

「那我去拿網子好嗎？」

「好啊！」

† 古巴人最崇仰的
　神聖守護者

其實根本就沒有魚網，小男孩記得，他們早就把網子賣掉了。但他們每天都要假裝演練一番，而且小男孩也知道，根本就沒有一鍋黃米飯和魚。

　　「八十五是一個吉利的數字，你看，我捕到了一條一千多磅重的魚回來，很高興吧！」老人說。

　　「我去拿網，然後再去拿沙丁魚。你到門口那裡去曬曬太陽，好不好？」

　　「好，這裡有昨天的報紙，我來看看棒球賽的新聞。」

　　小男孩不知道他所說的「昨天的報紙」，是不是也是假裝的，但老人的確從床底下取出了一份報紙。

　　老人解釋道：「這是我在鋪子時培里哥給我的。」

　　「我弄到沙丁魚後就回來。我會把你和我的沙丁魚一起冰起來，明天早上再來對分。我等一下回來，你可以跟我說球賽的新聞。」

　　「洋基不可能輸的。」

　　「但我怕克里夫蘭印地安人隊會贏。」

　　「孩子，你要對洋基有信心。你要想想，他們裡面有一個很厲害的狄馬喬。」

　　「底特律老虎隊和克里夫蘭印地安隊，這兩隊我都怕。」

　　「小心你連辛辛那提紅人隊和芝加哥白襪隊都要怕了！」

　　「你先讀新聞，等我回來再跟我說。」

「你覺得我們要不要買一張末尾是八十五的彩券，因為明天就是第八十五天。」

「可以是可以，但你最高的記錄是八十七天。」小男孩說。

「不可能再那麼倒楣了。你想你能買到末尾八十五的彩券嗎？」

「我可以指定一張。」

「一張要花兩塊半，我們要跟誰借錢？」

「那還不簡單，我隨時都可以借得到。」

「我想我也可以借得到，但我盡量不跟別人借錢，因為一旦借了錢，接下來就要乞討了。」

「你老人家不要著涼了，現在已經九月了。」小孩說。

「這是捕大魚的月分。」老人說：「在五月，誰都可以當漁夫。」

「我去撈沙丁魚了。」
小男孩說。

小男孩回來時，夕陽已經西下，老人坐在椅子上睡著了。男孩從床上拿起一條舊軍毯，鋪在椅背上，蓋著老人的肩膀。這是一對奇特的肩膀，雖然年紀很大了，依舊硬朗；脖子也很強健，老人垂著頭地睡著，頸背的皺紋沒那麼明顯。他的襯衫像船帆一樣，補了很多次的補釘，褪去的顏色被陽光照射得深淺不一。老人的臉看起來很老，他閉著眼睛，臉上看不出生命的氣息。徐徐的晚風吹來，他的膝蓋上攤著報紙，他用手臂壓著報紙，兩腳赤足。

　　男孩又離開了一會兒，等他再回來時，老人仍熟睡著。

　　「你老人家醒醒吧。」小男孩一邊說，一邊把手放在老人的膝蓋上。

　　老人睜開眼睛，這時才從睡夢裡醒過來。他露出笑容。

　　「你弄到了什麼東西？」他問。

　　小男孩說：「晚餐，我們要吃晚飯了。」

　　「我還不會很餓。」

　　「過來吃吧，你不能光捕魚，而不吃東西呀。」

　　「好。」老人說著，然後站起身，把報紙摺好，再把毯子摺疊起來。

　　「你就披著毯子吧！」小男孩說：「只要我還活著，我就不會讓你光捕魚，而沒吃東西。」

　　「那你就要好好照顧自己，活久一點。我們要吃什麼？」老人問。

「黑豆拌飯、炸香蕉,和一些燉肉。」

小男孩從露天酒店那裡用雙層的金屬飯盒裝了這些東西回來,他的口袋裡還有用紙巾包起來的兩組刀叉和湯匙。

「這些是誰給你的?」

「酒店的老闆,馬丁。」

「那我要好好謝謝他。」

「我已經謝過他了,你不需要再謝他了。」小男孩說。

「我會把大魚的肚子肉給他,他這樣免費請我們不只一次了吧?」老人說。

「應該是吧!」

「那除了給他魚肚肉,還要再多給他一點其他的部分,他對我們實在是太慷慨了。」老人說。

「他還送我們兩瓶啤酒。」

「我最喜歡罐裝的啤酒啦。」

「我知道,但這是瓶裝的哈土依啤酒,瓶子我會拿回去還。」

「你真好,我們開動吧!」老人說。

小男孩輕聲地說:「我一直在等你呢,在你還沒準備好之前,我不想先打開飯盒。」

「我已經準備好了,我只要去洗一下手就可以了。」

你要去哪裡洗呀?小男孩心裡想,村子供水的地方,走過去還要過兩條街,我應該帶水過來給他的,還要弄塊香皂和一條好的毛巾來。我怎麼這麼粗心？我還得弄件襯衫和夾克，好讓他過冬，另外再弄雙鞋子和一條毯子。」

「這燉肉很好吃。」老人說。

「跟我說球賽的新聞吧！」小男孩央求老人道。

「我說過的，在美國聯盟中只有洋基隊才夠看。」老人興奮地說道。

「但他們今天輸了。」小男孩告訴老人說。

「那不代表什麼，偉大的狄馬喬會重振雄風的。」

「他們隊裡還有其他的隊員。」

「話是沒錯，但有他就不同了。另一個聯盟，像布魯克

林隊和費城隊，我就比較喜歡布魯克林隊，不過，我也忘不了狄克‧席斯勒在舊球場上的精彩演出。」

「他無人可及，沒看過有人可以打出比他更遠的球。」

「你記不記得他以前常到露天酒店來？我想邀他一塊去捕魚，不過我不好意思開口，就叫你去問他，結果你也不意思問。」

「記得啊，我們真是錯失了大好機會。如果他跟我們去捕魚，那我們會畢生難忘。」

「我想找偉大的狄馬喬去捕魚，聽說他父親也是漁夫，搞不好也曾經和我們一樣窮，可以瞭解我們的好意。」

「不過偉大的席斯勒的父親，就沒有窮過了。他父親在我這個年紀的時候，就在打大聯盟了。」

「我像你這麼大的時候，在專跑非洲的橫帆船上當水手。我還曾在傍晚時在海灘上看過獅子。」

「我知道，你跟我說過。」

「我們要聊非洲，還是聊棒球？」

小男孩說：「我想聊棒球，告訴我，偉大的約翰‧J‧馬格魯怎麼樣了？」他把「J」唸成了「荷達」。

「他以前有時也會來露天酒店，不過他酒品很差，喝醉酒就會滿口粗話，很難搞。他心裡只想著賽馬和棒球，起碼他的口袋裡都會帶著賽馬的名單，而且在講電話時，常常開口閉口都是馬的名字。」

「他是個偉大的教頭，我爸覺得他是最好的教頭。」小男孩說。

「那是因為他常到這裡來，如果杜瑞奇也是每年持續到這裡來的話，你爸也會說他是最偉大的教頭。」老人說。

「那到底誰才是最偉大的教頭？是魯克，還是麥克·岡札列茲？」

「我想他們兩個人差不多！」

「那最偉大的漁夫就是你了。」

「才不是，我認識比我更厲害的漁夫。」

「才怪！」小男孩說：「是有一些厲害的漁夫，偉大的漁夫也有一些，不過像你這樣的就只有一個。」

「謝謝，你這樣說我很高興。希望不要來了一條我對付不來的大魚，以免砸了招牌。」

「只要你還像你所說的那樣體力很好的話，就沒有你對付不了的魚。」

「搞不好我的體力已經大不如前了，不過我的捕魚訣竅很多，而且毅力過人。」老人說。

「你現在該上床休息了，這樣明天一早精神才會好。我把這些東西送回露天酒店。」

「那麼晚安了，我明天早上會去叫醒你。」

「你是我的鬧鐘。」小男孩說。

「年齡是我的鬧鐘。老人家為什麼會那麼早起？這樣就會覺得一天比較長嗎？」老人說。

「我不曉得，我只知道年輕的男生都睡得很晚，爬不起來。」小男孩說。

「我會記住，準時把你叫醒的。」老人說。

「我不喜歡他來叫醒我，因為這樣子好像我很沒用。」

「我瞭解。」

「你老人家好好睡吧！」

小男孩走了出去。他們在沒有燈光的桌上吃完晚餐，老人摸黑脫下長褲，上床睡覺。他把褲子捲起來，然後在裡頭塞上報紙，當作枕頭，接著蜷縮在毛毯裡，躺在用舊報紙鋪著的彈簧床上。

他很快就入睡。他夢到了非洲，那時他還是個男孩，夢裡綿延著金黃色的海灘，還有白得刺眼的白色海灘，以及高聳的海岬和崢嶸的棕色山脈。他現在每晚都會夢到這個海岸，聽著海浪的波濤聲，看著當地土人駕著船，穿梭在海面上。在睡夢中，他還可以聞到甲板上的焦油味、填塞船縫的麻絮味，還有清晨微風吹過非洲大地的氣味。

　　通常他一嗅到陸地吹來的微風，便會醒來，穿好衣服去叫醒小男孩。但今晚從陸地那邊來的風很早就吹過來，他在睡夢中知道時候還早，所以就讓自己繼續夢下去。接著，他夢見海島的白色峰頂由海上浮起，看到加那利群島的各個港口和下錨處。

　　他不再夢見暴風雨，不再夢見女人，不再夢見什麼大事件，不再夢見大魚、爭執、和人比腕力，也不再夢見妻子。他現在只會夢到各個地方，還有海灘上的獅子；這些獅子像小貓一樣在黃昏中嬉戲，他很喜歡這些獅子，就像他很喜歡小男孩一樣。不過，他沒有夢過小男孩。他清醒過來，往敞開的門外望了一下月亮，然後把捲起的褲子攤開、穿上。他到屋外小便後，就沿著路走去叫醒小男孩。清晨的寒氣讓他打哆嗦，他知道多抖幾下可以暖和點，而且他很快就要划船了。

　　小男孩住的房子，門沒有上鎖。他打開門，赤足地悄聲走進去。小男孩睡在第一個房間的小床上，老人可以就著外面微弱的月光，清楚地看見小男孩。他輕輕地握住小男孩的一隻腳，直到小男孩醒過來、轉身看到老人。老人向他點了個頭，小男孩於是從床邊的椅子上拿起褲子，坐在床邊，把褲子穿上。

　　老人走出門外，小男孩尾隨著老人。小男孩還睡眼惺忪，老人把手放在男孩的肩膀上說：「抱歉。」

　　「沒事，」小男孩說，「男子漢就是要這樣。」

他們沿著路，來到老人的小屋。黑暗中，一路上有許多打著赤腳的男人，扛著船槳往前走。

老人和小男孩來到小屋後，小男孩拿起籃裡成捲的魚線、魚叉和魚鉤，老人則拿起捲帆的船槳，扛在肩上。

「你要喝咖啡嗎？」小男孩問。

「我們先把工具放到船上，然後再回來弄點喝的。」

他們來到一個專供漁夫早餐的地方，用煉乳的罐子喝咖啡。

「你昨晚睡得好不好？」小男孩問。小男孩雖然還很想睡，但現在已經漸漸醒了過來。

「我睡得很好，馬諾林。我今天很有信心。」老人說。

「我也是。我現在去拿我們的沙丁魚，還有你的新鮮魚餌。他都自己拿工具，不讓別人碰他的東西。」

老人說：「我們不一樣，你五歲時我就讓你拿東西了。」

「對啊。我快去快回，你再喝一杯咖啡吧！反正這裡我們可以賒帳。」小男孩說。

他離開，赤腳踩在珊瑚礁上，走去貯存魚餌的冰庫。

老人慢慢啜飲咖啡，因為一整天下來，他只有這點東西可以吃，所以他知道他應該多喝點。他已經好一段時間嫌吃東西很麻煩了，所以他不帶午餐，只在船頭放一瓶水，然後就這樣過一整天。

老人與海

　　這時小男孩回來了，他把沙丁魚和兩個魚餌包在報紙裡，然後兩人踩著鵝卵石沙地，沿著小路走向小船。接著他們抬起小船，把船推入水裡去。

　　「祝你好運。」

　　「也祝你好運。」老人說。他把船槳的繩索套在槳座上固定，然後將槳葉片插入水裡，身體往前傾斜，在黑暗中划出海港。這時也有從其他海灘出海的船隻，雖然月亮已經落到山的另一頭，老人看不到那些船，但可以聽到其他船槳下水和划水的聲音。

　　有時候，可以聽到別的船上傳來的說話聲，但大部分的船除了划槳的聲音外，一片寂靜。出了港口之後，船隻各分東西，去他們認為可以捕到魚的地方。老人知道他會划到很遠的地方，把土地的氣息留在後方，迎向清晨海洋的清新空氣。他划到漁夫所說的「深井」海洋地帶，那裡有一個七百噚†深的海溝，可以看見海灣裡的海草所發出的燐光；由於海潮沖激著海底陡峭的石牆，造成漩渦，因此各類的魚群都匯聚在此。另外還有蝦子、做魚餌用的魚，有時候還有一群群的烏賊，都會聚集在深洞裡。到了晚上，牠們會游到海面上，成為附近魚群的食物。

---

　　† 噚（fathom），英美等國的長度計算單位，
　　　一噚約為1.8288公尺。

在黑暗中，老人可以感覺到黎明已近。划船時，他聽見了飛魚離開水面，劃破黑暗天際時的顫抖聲，以及堅硬的翅膀所發出的噗噗聲。他喜歡飛魚，因為牠們是他在大海中最好的朋友。他同情鳥兒，尤其是那些總是在飛翔，卻幾乎永遠找不到食物的纖小黑燕鷗。他想，除了那些專門靠掠奪為生、又大又強壯的鳥外，其他的鳥都過著比人類還困苦的生活。為什麼造物者要把鳥創造得如此纖弱，像是海燕，而卻把海洋造得如此殘酷？海洋仁慈而美麗，卻也可以瞬間變得殘酷，讓那些潛入海中捕食的飛鳥，在微弱的哀鳴聲中被大海所吞噬。

　　他一直把海洋叫做「海娘子」，在西班牙文裡，人們喜歡她時都這麼稱呼。那些喜歡海洋的人，有時也會咒罵她，口氣上把她當成女人。有些年輕的漁夫們，他們把浮標當作魚線的浮子，等到靠賣鯊魚肝賺到足夠的錢，就可以去買馬達汽艇，他們把海洋叫做男性化的「海郎」。他們之所以這麼稱呼，是因為把大海視為競爭的對手、地點或敵人。可是老人都把海洋當成女人，有時施予恩惠，有時又拒絕給予，反覆無常。如果她狂嘯怒號，那也是身不由己。老人認為，月亮會影響海水的潮汐，就如同影響女人的情緒一樣。

他平穩地划著船，由於速度都保持一定，所以並不費力，除了偶爾會有海流的漩渦外，大部分的時候都是風平浪靜。藉助海浪的推力，他可以少花三分之一的力氣。破曉時分，他已經划得比預期的還要遠了。

他想，在「深井」快一個星期了，卻一無所獲。今天一定要到鰹魚和青花魚出沒的地點，那裡搞不好會有大魚！在天還沒完全亮以前，他隨著水流，把所有的魚餌都放下水。第一個魚餌垂到四十噚深，第二個魚餌放到七十五噚深的地方，第三個和第四個分別放到一百噚和一百二十五噚深的深藍色海水中。每一個魚餌都和魚鉤捆綁得很緊，鉤子的上端整個藏在魚餌裡，鉤子彎曲和尖尖的部分，用新鮮的沙丁魚包覆起來，從每一條沙丁魚的雙眼穿過，沿著鋼鉤形成一個像半圓形的花環，這樣會讓大魚以為整個魚鉤的任何一部份都很鮮美可口。

小孩給他兩條新鮮的小鮪魚和青花魚，他把牠們綁在兩條垂得最深的魚線上，就像綁在錘線上的鉛錘一樣。其他的鉤子，掛上了一條之前用過而未腐壞的大西洋藍鰺和黃魚，更何況還有鮮美誘人的沙丁魚。每一條魚線都有大鉛筆這麼粗，上面綁著綠色的小樹枝，只要魚餌被拉動或碰觸到，樹枝便會往下沉。每一條魚線都會有兩捲四十噚長的線，可以隨時和其他備用的線連接，在必要時，有三百噚長的線預留給魚拖走。

老人這時守著船邊的三根小樹枝，等待它們往下沉。他慢慢划著船，讓魚線保持垂直，垂進適當的深度中。這時天已經很亮了，太陽隨時就會升起。

太陽漸漸從海平面升起，老人能看到其他的船隻隨著海水起伏，朝海岸的方向、順著潮流撒出網子。陽光越來越亮，當太陽完全升起時，海水反射著耀眼的陽光，波光再反射到他的眼睛，讓他一時睜不開眼來。他盡量避開陽光划船，看著水中的魚線是否垂直落在深邃幽暗的海面下。沒有人的釣線能垂得像他那麼直，這樣潮流暗處的不同深淺之處，都會準確地垂著魚餌，等待游過那裡的魚前來上鉤。別的漁夫通常都是讓魚餌隨波逐流，有時魚餌只停在六十噚深，卻以為深及一百噚。

老人心想，我下餌都盡量算得精確，只是運氣不好罷了。可是天曉得，或許今天就走運也說不定，每天都是新的開始。運氣好固然不錯，但我寧願算得精準，因為當機會來臨時，我就有萬全的準備了。

兩個小時後，太陽升得更高了，朝東方看去，不再那麼刺眼。現在老人的視線範圍內，只有三艘船，而這些船彷彿都低於海平面下，且離岸邊很近。

他想，我這一輩子，總是讓早晨的陽光刺痛眼睛，不過我視力還很好，黃昏時甚至可以直視太陽，眼前也不會發黑。其實傍晚的陽光更強，但早上的陽光讓人感到不適。

就在此時，他看到一隻蒼鷹，伸展著黑色的長翅膀，在他頭頂上空盤旋。突然間，那隻鳥倏地傾斜翅膀飛掠海面，接著打個轉又盤旋了起來。

老人大聲地說：「牠一定抓到了什麼東西，而不光是看看而已。」

他平穩緩慢地划到鳥盤旋的地方，不急不徐地將魚線保持上下垂直。他設法划得比潮流的速度快，這樣才能準確地捕到魚。如果不是為了想利用這隻鳥來捕魚，老人是不會划這麼快的。

鳥飛得更高了，接著在空中盤旋了幾圈，翅膀保持不動，突然之間，才往下俯衝。老人看見飛魚從水中躍出，迅速地掠過水面。

「鯕鰍，大鯕鰍！」老人大聲地叫著。

他擱下船槳，從船頭下拿起一根細釣絲。釣絲上有一段鐵絲線和中型魚鉤，他在鉤子上掛上沙丁魚餌，沿著船緣垂進水裡，然後將魚線固定在船尾的環狀螺拴上。他又在另一條釣絲上裝好魚餌，繞成一圈垂入船頭的陰影處，隨後拾起槳開始划船，望著那隻長翼的黑鳥，正低低地飛掠水面，尋覓食物。

正看得出神時，鳥傾斜著翅膀，再度俯衝水面，猛烈卻徒勞無功地振翅，追逐著飛魚。就在此時，老人可以看見大鯕鰍追逐著落荒而逃的飛魚，在後面掀起小小的波浪。鯕鰍正好在飛魚跳躍水面時，在下面游過，當飛魚落入水裡，便給鯕鰍逮個正著。老人心想，好多鯕鰍，鯕鰍到處都是，飛魚根本就沒有逃命的機會。因為飛魚身軀太大，速度也太快，所以鳥很難叼到飛魚。

　　他看著飛魚一再從水裡跳躍而出，看著鳥不斷徒勞無功地撲向水面。老人心想：「鯕鰍已經離我遠去，牠們游得又快又遠。不過我或許能在其中找到一條落單的大魚，我的大魚一定就在某個地方。」

　　陸地上的雲彩飄得和山巒同高，海岸成了一條長長的綠線，背後襯托著灰藍色的小山丘，海水一片深藍色，藍得幾乎發紫。他往水裡看去，只見到紅色的微生物在黝暗的海水中漂浮，映照著陽光，反射出奇異的光輝。他注視著筆直垂入水中的魚線沒入不見。老人很高興看到那麼多浮游微生物，這代表附近有魚。太陽升得更高了，陽光在水中呈現奇異的光彩，還有陸地上空雲彩的形狀，都表示今天是個大晴天。那隻蒼鷹已消失無蹤，海面上無一物，除了幾堆被太陽曬得變了色的黃色馬尾藻，還有一隻完整、全身泛著彩虹光暈的紫色膠質僧帽水母。水母漂浮在船旁邊，翻了個身後像氣泡一樣，輕鬆愉快地在水中飄浮著，

有毒的紫色長觸鬚，在身後拖了有一碼長的距離。

「賤貨，婊子！」老人罵道。

他輕輕搖著槳，朝水裡望去，水裡有一些小魚，顏色和水母的觸鬚相同，這些小魚穿梭在水母的觸鬚間，悠游在漂浮的氣泡陰影下。小魚們根本不在乎觸鬚上的劇毒，但人類卻不然，老人在釣魚時，釣絲上偶爾會沾上一些黏膩膩的紫色觸鬚，如果手碰到了這些東西，手臂和手便會又腫又痛，就好像摸到有毒的常春藤和橡樹一樣。只不過這些賤貨的毒性發作得很快，就像鞭子抽下來那麼迅速。

那些彩虹般的氣泡非常美麗，但它們是海洋中最虛偽的東西。老人很喜歡看大海龜吃氣泡的模樣，海龜一看到氣泡，便會趨向前去，閉上眼睛，整個身體縮進殼內，把氣泡連同觸鬚一起吃掉，老人喜歡看海龜吃掉氣泡的樣子。暴風雨過後，老人也喜歡在沙灘上踏著牠們的身體，聆聽腳底的厚繭踩在海龜背上時，龜殼所發出的劈啪迸裂聲。

老人很喜歡綠海龜和玳瑁，牠們體態優雅，動作敏捷，而且很值錢。不過對於巨大又笨拙的蠵龜，老人就帶著善意的輕蔑，因為牠們雖然全副武裝，卻懦弱地縮在龜殼裡；牠們交配時的姿勢陰陽怪氣，而且會閉著眼睛、愉悅地吃著僧帽水母。

老人在捕龜船上待過許多年，但他不覺得海龜有什麼神秘。他同情所有的海龜，甚至對那將近一噸重、軀幹像小船一樣長的海龜感到憐憫。大多數人對海龜都很殘忍，因為把海龜剖殺後，牠的心臟還可以繼續跳動好幾個小時。但老人想，我也有那樣一顆心臟，四肢也像牠們一樣。老人從五月就開始吃白色的海龜蛋來增強體力，這樣一直持續到九、十月，才有足夠的力氣去捕捉真正的大魚。

他每天還要喝一杯鯊魚肝油，在漁夫貯放工具的小屋裡，他們放了一大桶鯊魚肝油，想喝的漁夫都可以去那裡拿。大部分的漁夫都不喜歡魚肝油的味道，不過這倒也不比摸黑早起來得令人痛恨，況且魚肝油可以預防傷風感冒，而且對眼睛很好。

這時，老人抬頭望去，看見那隻鳥又再度在空中盤旋。

「牠找到魚了。」老人大聲說。沒有飛魚跳出水面，魚餌也沒有散開，老人只看到一條小鮪魚躍到半空中，一轉身，頭朝下落入水裡。那條鮪魚在陽光下閃著銀光，牠跳下水後，接著又有幾條鮪魚躍出水面，從四面八方跳躍，

跳得很遠，把海水拍得劈啪響。牠們繞著釣餌兜圈子，追趕著魚餌。

老人心想，要不是鮪魚游得那麼快，我就可以趕上牠們。他看著鮪魚把海水攪動得白花花的，蒼鷹趁機俯衝下來啄食，因為小鮪魚已經嚇得驚慌地翻滾出水面。

「這隻鳥幫了大忙。」老人說。這時，拴在船尾、壓在他腳下的釣線突然拉緊，他擱下槳，抓緊釣絲，開始收線。他能感受到小鮪魚顫抖地掙扎，他越往上拉，魚抖得越厲害，老人先看到魚在水中的藍色背脊和金黃色的兩側，隨後把牠甩過船舷摔到船上。陽光照射著，魚躺在船尾，身體結實得像一枚子彈，瞪著呆滯的大眼睛。牠被重重地摔在船板上時，尾巴仍靈巧快速地拍打著。老人不忍看牠受苦，便在牠頭上猛敲了一記，又踢了幾腳，可是那條魚依然在船尾陰影處抖動著身體。

「青花魚用來做餌，太棒了，這隻有十來磅重吧。」老人大聲說。

他不記得什麼時候養成了大聲自言自語的習慣。以前沒有人在旁邊時，他會唱歌自娛，有時候一個人在小漁船或捕龜船上值更時，也會哼哼唱唱。大概是小男孩離開後，孤伶伶一個人，才開始大聲的自言自語，但他記不清楚了。其實當老人和小孩一起捕魚時，除非必要，不然也不太說話，只有夜晚或被暴風雨困住時才會聊天。在海上不

講廢話是一種美德，這是老人的信念，他一直謹守這種行規。但現在沒有人在旁邊，不怕干擾別人，想到什麼便大聲說出來。

「如果讓別人聽到我在大聲地自言自語，一定會以為我是個瘋子。不過，反正我又不是瘋子，管別人怎麼說。哪像那些有錢人，船上還有收音機對著他們講話，播報球賽新聞。」他又大聲地說。

現在沒時間去想棒球賽了，他現在只能想一件事，就是我生下來是要做什麼的。他想，也許在那群魚中，會有一條大魚，我只是從那群捕食的青花魚中，抓一條落單的，可是牠們游得太快太遠了。今天海面上的魚都往東北方游去，而且速度很快。難道是因為時辰的關係，還是一種我不知道的天氣預兆？

此時老人已經看不到岸邊的青綠色，只能看見青色的山頂隱約覆蓋著白雪，還有雪山似的雲層高聳在青山之外。海水深暗，陽光在水裡映照出斑斕的虹彩，斑點狀的浮游生物變化出萬點霞光，在高昇的陽光照射下消逝。現在老人唯一看到的，是釣絲筆直垂入蔚藍海水所發出的光影。

鮪魚又沉入海水中了。漁夫把這一類魚全叫做鮪魚，只有在出售或用來換取魚餌時，才會叫牠們真正的名稱。現在，老人可以感到灼熱的陽光曬在頸背上，划槳時，汗珠沿著背脊落下。

他想，我可以任船漂流，好好睡一覺，將釣絲套在腳指頭上，這樣一有動靜就會把我驚醒的。不過今天是第八十五天了，應該會大有收穫才對。

　　老人看著釣絲，這時，他看見綠色桿子倏然往下墜落。

　　「有了，有了。」他說。老人小心翼翼地擱好槳，以免震動小船。他伸手抓住釣絲，輕輕夾在右手的大拇指和食指間，他感到釣絲的另一端沒有拉力也沒有重量，握在手上很輕鬆。他把釣線又往下拉了一下，不過這只是試探一下，拉得並也不用力。老人很清楚牠在打什麼主意。在下面一百噚深的海裡，有一條馬林魚正在享用覆蓋在鉤尖和鉤柄上的沙丁魚餌，手工錘成的釣鉤也掛上一條小鮪魚。

　　老人靈巧地握住釣線，用左手輕輕地將釣絲從桿子上解下來。現在，他可以用手指慢慢把線拉回來，不讓那條馬林魚察覺到而感到緊張。

　　離岸這麼遠，又在這個月份，一定是條大魚。老人心想，吃吧，魚兒，盡量吃吧，那些沙丁魚很鮮美可口。你到下面深達六百呎黑暗的冷水裡，兜一圈後再回來吃吧。

　　老人感到一陣輕微的拉力，緊接著又猛拉一下，一定是沙丁魚餌的頭很難從鉤子上扯下來。接著，又沒了動靜。

　　「快點來呀！轉一圈，聞聞看，那些沙丁魚多美味呀，現在好好吃掉吧。還有鮪魚呢，又肥又冷又可口，不要害羞，魚兒，快來吃吧。」老人大聲說。

　　他等待著，用大拇指和食指捏著釣絲，一邊注意這根釣絲，一邊還要盯著其他釣絲，因為這條魚可能會上下游動。然後，又一陣輕輕地拉曳。

　　老人又自言自語，「牠一定會吃魚餌，老天爺幫幫忙，讓牠吃魚餌吧！」

　　然而那條魚並沒有吃魚餌，牠溜走了，老人渾然不察。

　　「牠不可能溜走，老天爺知道牠不會跑掉，只是轉個圈罷了。牠以前大概上過鉤，記得慘痛的教訓。」老人說。

　　老人又感到釣絲輕輕動了一下，高興極了。

　　「牠剛才只是兜兜圈子，一定會上鉤的。」他說。

　　他很高興感到一陣輕輕的拉力。接著，他感覺底下猛烈一拉，力量大得嚇人，那是魚的重量！老人鬆手讓釣絲慢慢放下去，再放下去，兩捲預備用的釣線已經放完一捲。釣線輕輕從指縫間滑過，但他仍能感受到那條魚很重，儘管他的大拇指和食指施加的壓力簡直小得難以察覺。

　　「好大一條魚啊！牠現在橫啣著魚餌在游動。」他說。

　　老人心想，牠會打個轉，然後把餌吃下去。他沒有把這話說出來，因為好事一旦說出口，可能就不會實現。他知道這是一條大魚，他能想像那傢伙把魚餌橫啣在嘴裡，在黑暗中游開的樣子。這時，老人感覺到魚靜止不動，但重量仍在那裡。接著，重量逐漸加重，他把釣線又放長了些，用力地將釣線捏緊在拇指和食指間。下面的重量又猛然加重，並且筆直地往下沉。

「上鉤了，現在我要讓牠好好享受一頓。」老人說。

他讓釣線繼續從手中放出去，然後一邊伸出左手，拿起兩捲備用的線頭，連接在另外一根釣絲上。老人現在一切準備就緒，除了手邊正在使用的這捲線之外，還有三捲四十噚長的備用釣線。

他說，「再多吃一點吧，好好地吃吧。」

他心想，好好地吃吧，讓魚鉤戳進你的心臟，你就一命嗚呼了。然後再乖乖地浮上來，我才好把魚叉戳進你身體。好了，你準備好了嗎？這頓飯你也吃得夠久了吧！

老人大聲地說：「就是現在了。」他用雙手使勁地拉，總算將魚線往上拉了一碼長，然後左右手交替用力往後拉，使盡手臂的力氣和全身的重量。

不過他並沒有拉動那條魚。那條魚自顧慢慢地游開，老人連拉牠一吋的距離都拉不動。他的釣線很強韌，是專門用來捕大魚的。他把釣線繞到身體背後往上拖，由於線拉得很緊，一顆顆水珠從釣線上迸下來，在水裡發出緩慢的嘶嘶聲。老人仍然緊握著釣線，他把身體靠在船板上，身子往後仰，抵抗魚往前拉的力量，這時小船也緩緩地朝西北方移動。

那條魚不慌不忙地游著，魚、船和人，在平靜無波的海上緩緩移動。其餘的魚餌仍留在水中，可是老人已經顧不了那麼多了。

老人自言自語道：「如果小男孩在就好了，我竟被一條魚拖著跑，身體成了繫繩的短樁。我可以把釣線固定住，不過這樣魚就會把線扯斷。我要全力抓住牠，在必要時才放線。謝天謝地，牠是繼續往前游，而不是向下鑽。」

如果牠往下鑽，我就不知道該怎麼處理了。如果牠潛入海底死了，我也會束手無策。但我要想個辦法，能用的方法有很多。

老人握緊繞在背上的釣線，看著釣線斜入水中，小船穩定地朝西北方移動。

再這樣下去牠活不了的，老人想，牠總不能永遠這樣撐下去吧。然而四個小時之後，那條魚依然穩定地拖著小船游向大海，老人緊緊地抓住繞在背上的釣線，不敢鬆懈。

「牠是中午的時候上鉤的，到現在為止，我還沒看到牠現身。」老人說。

在還沒釣到這條魚之前，他把草帽往前額壓得低低的，現在前額都有深深的痕印了。他口也渴了，於是彎下膝蓋，盡量小心不要拉動釣線。他靠近船頭，伸手把水瓶拿過來，打開喝了幾口，然後靠在船頭上小憩片刻。他坐在橫擺的桅杆船帆旁休息，什麼都不去想，只是耐心等待。

之後老人回頭望一眼，已經看不見陸地了。他想，也沒什麼關係，可以藉著哈瓦那的燈火回去。離太陽下山還有兩個小時，也許在太陽下山之前，魚會浮出水面；如果沒

有的話，可能會和月亮一起出現；再不然，等明天太陽升起，就會浮出水面了。我的手腳沒有抽筋，體力還很好，況且嘴巴被鉤子鉤住的是牠。不過，能這樣拖著船跑的魚應該很大，牠一定是緊閉嘴咬著釣線，真想能看看牠的樣子，哪怕只是看一眼也好，好讓我知道這位對手是誰。

老人從星象得知，這條魚整晚都沒有改變航線和方向。太陽下山後，溫度降低，老人的背、雙臂和衰老腿上的汗，冷得風乾了。白天，他把蓋在餌盒的袋子攤開在陽光下晾曬，太陽下山後，他把袋子纏在脖子上，垂到背後，小心翼翼地將袋子墊在釣線下。袋子緩和了釣線的壓力，他盡可能傾身往船頭靠，這樣會比較舒服些。其實，這個姿勢只是比較不那麼難受而已，但他覺得已經很舒適了。

老人想，我對牠一點辦法都沒有，牠對我也莫可奈何，再這樣下去，對誰都沒有好處。

他站起來，對著船邊外撒了泡尿。他望著星斗，研判航行的方向。釣線像一條燐光線，從他的肩膀直直地垂入水中。船緩慢地移動，哈瓦那的燈光沒那麼強了，他判斷潮流把船帶往東邊了。他想，如果看不到哈瓦那的燈火，那方向就會更偏東。魚的方向如果不變，應該還有好幾個小時可以看到岸上的燈火。他想，不知道今天大聯盟的球賽結果如何，要是有台收音機該有多好。然後他又想，每次都是想想罷了，還是想想現在的正事，不要做蠢事。

接著，他大聲地說：「如果小男孩在旁邊幫忙就好了，而且他也可以見識見識這個場面。」

他想，人老了是不應該孤伶伶的，但這也是無可奈何的事。我要記得在鮪魚還沒壞掉之前吃一些來保持體力。要記住，不管多麼沒有胃口，早上一定要吃點東西。千萬要記得，他對自己這麼叮嚀。

晚上，一對鼠海豚游到船邊來，老人可以聽到牠們翻滾和噴水的聲音。他可以分辨出雄的鼠海豚發出的噴水聲，和雌的鼠海豚發出嘆息聲。

「牠們多乖，玩鬧在一起，非常恩愛，牠們和飛魚一樣，都是我們的兄弟。」他說。

　　然後，他又開始憐憫起那條已經上鉤的大魚。他想，牠真是了不起，很神奇，可是誰知道牠的年紀有多大？我沒見過這麼強悍的魚，也沒遇過行徑這麼古怪的魚。牠應該是太聰明了，所以不跳。牠要是跳起來或猛撞一下，那會要了我的命。不過牠以前可能多次上過鉤，知道用這種方法來抵抗最有效。不過，牠不會知道對手只有我一個人，而且是一個老頭子。這條魚可真大呀，如果魚肉夠好，可以拿去市場上賣。牠吃魚餌的樣子像條公魚，拉動釣線的樣子，也像條公魚，在這場戰鬥中不驚不慌。不知道牠究竟是胸有成竹，還是跟我一樣被逼得非背水一戰不可？

　　老人想起那次在一對馬林魚中，釣起雌魚的情形。雄魚都會讓雌魚先吃，上了鉤的雌魚驚慌絕望地掙扎，把體力消耗殆盡。而那條雄魚一直繞著雌魚打轉，在釣線附近穿梭，躍出水面。由於雄魚靠得很近，老人擔心牠會用尾巴將釣線剪斷，牠的尾巴很鋒利，大小和形狀都像鐮刀。老人用魚叉刺起雌魚，再用棍棒敲打，握住有如長劍、邊緣像粗砂紙一樣的嘴巴，朝牠的頭敲下去，直到頭的顏色變成像鏡子背面一樣的赭紅色。然後小男孩幫忙把魚拖到船上去，而那條雄魚還在小船附近徘徊。後來，當老人在整理釣線和魚叉時，雄魚竟然跳到空中，俯視雌魚在什麼地方，再鑽回海裡，牠淡紫色的羽翼——胸鰭張開來，寬條紋一覽無遺。老人依稀記得牠很漂亮，徘徊捨不得離去。

老人心想，那是我見過最令人傷心的事了，小男孩也很難過。我們祈求雌魚原諒，然後迅速地將牠切割開來。

「真希望小男孩在這裡。」老人大聲地自言自語。他靠在船頭的圓柱上，透過肩膀上的魚線，他可以感覺到大魚的重量，而大魚仍穩定地朝著牠要走的方向前進。

牠一旦中了我的圈套，就非得想辦法不可了，老人想。

牠的辦法是潛伏在深暗的海底裡，讓這些陷阱、圈套和詭計都奈何不了牠，而我的辦法則是到人跡罕至的地方，再把牠揪出來。從我們互相遭遇開始，從中午一直到現在，都沒有第三者來幫我們解決僵局。

我大概是不應該打漁的，他想。不過，我生下來就是要幹這一行。天亮之前，我要記得吃一點鮪魚來維持體力。

在破曉前不久，有什麼東西咬掉了老人後方的魚餌。他聽到桿子折斷的聲音，釣線沿著船緣被拖走。老人摸黑從刀鞘中抽出小刀，身子往後靠，把魚拉扯的力量移到左肩來承擔。他摸黑把最靠近的另外一根釣線也切斷，連同船沿邊割斷被拖走的釣線，把兩條線打死結連接起來。他很有技巧地只用單手進行，一腳踩住線圈，一手把結繫緊。現在他有六捲備用釣線，被他切斷的魚餌有兩捲備用線，那條上鉤的魚也有兩捲備用線，這些釣線都連接了起來。

他想，等天亮後要設法往後移，把四十噚深的餌線切斷，再和預備線連接起來，這樣我可能會損失兩百噚長高

級的卡特蘭釣線和釣鉤。不過，這些損失是可以補回來的，但如果讓這條大魚溜掉的話，那就補不回來了。剛才咬掉魚餌的，不知是哪一種魚，可能是條馬林魚，也可能是箭魚或鯊魚，我還來不及去想，就太快放手了。

他大聲地說：「要是小男孩在這就好了。」

不過小男孩並不在身邊，老人想。你只有孤伶伶一人，現在還是乖乖地把最後那根釣線處理好吧。不管還是不是天黑，趕快把它切斷，把這兩捲預備線也連接起來。

於是他開始行動，在黑暗中進行很困難。這時，那條魚突然掀起一陣大浪，把他拖倒了。他臉朝下，眼睛下方摔出了一道傷口。鮮血沿著老人的臉頰流下，在還沒流到下巴前，就凝結乾了。他走回船頭，靠在木板上休息。他調整一下肩膀上的袋子，小心地把壓在肩上的釣線挪開，換到肩膀的另一個部位，然後用肩膀支撐住。老人小心地試探魚的動靜，並把手伸到水中，感覺一下船行的速度。

他想，不知道牠為什麼要掀起這陣風浪，可能是釣線從牠高如小山的背脊滑過。當然，牠的背不會像我的背那樣疼痛。不過，無論牠多麼強大，總不可能一輩子拖著小船跑吧。現在會造成問題的東西我都處理了，我還有一大捲的預備線，一個人所能要求的也只有這麼多了。

「魚啊，我到死都要陪著你。」老人溫柔地大聲說。

牠也會一直陪著我，老人想。他等待著天亮，破曉前，寒氣襲人，他緊貼著木板取暖。他想，牠能撐多久，我就能撐多久。第一道陽光露出，釣線往外延伸垂入水中，小船穩定地移動。這時，太陽從老人的右肩方向升起。

　　老人說：「牠往北邊游。」海流會把我們沖向遠遠的東方，他想。希望牠會順著海潮游，這表示牠已經累了。

　　太陽升得更高了，老人知道那條魚一點都不累。而唯一比較有利的現象是，釣線的傾斜度顯示牠已經游到較淺的地方。這並不表示牠一定會跳起來，不過，牠很有可能會跳起來。

「老天爺個忙，讓牠跳起來，我有足夠的釣線可以應付牠。」老人說。

他想，只要把釣線再拉緊一點，弄痛牠，牠可能就會跳起來。現在，天色整個亮了，讓牠跳吧，那麼牠背脊骨旁的氣囊便會充滿空氣，這樣就不會沉入海底死在那裡了。

他想把釣線收緊一點，可是大魚上鉤後，釣線已經繃得快斷了。他身體往後傾斜，感到釣線有強勁的反應，無法再用力拉動，他知道已經沒辦法把釣線再拉得更緊了。他想，我還是不要硬拉，因為每拉扯一次，魚鉤鉤住魚嘴的裂口就會變得更大，這樣當牠跳起來時，很容易就會把魚鉤給甩掉。反正太陽出來後，我感覺好一些了，至少我不必注視著牠。

釣線黏著黃色的海草，老人很高興，因為他知道這樣大魚會更難拖動船。那是墨西哥灣黃色的海草，在黑夜裡發出燐光。

「魚啊，我愛你，也很尊敬你，但我一定要在天黑以前把你解決掉。」他說。

但願如此，他想。

一隻小鳥從北方朝小船飛來，那是一隻鳴禽，沿著水面低低地飛著。老人可以感覺出小鳥很疲倦。

鳥飛向船尾，歇息了一會兒，然後在老人頭頂上盤旋，最後停在釣線上面，在那裡會比較舒適些。

老人問鳥：「你多大？這時你第一次離家出遠門嗎？」

他在說話時，鳥望著他。鳥太累了，還來不及檢查釣線穩不穩，細小的腳爪便緊抓著釣絲晃來晃去。

「釣絲很穩的，太穩啦。」老人告訴牠：「昨晚沒有風，你不應該那麼累的，鳥啊，你是怎麼搞的？」

他想，一定會有蒼鷹出海捕捉小鳥，但他並沒有叮嚀小鳥，反正牠也聽不懂老人說的話，更何況不用多久，小鳥很快就會得到蒼鷹給牠的教訓了。

「鳥兒，好好休息吧。然後再出發去碰碰運氣，不管是人、是鳥、是魚，不都一樣嗎？」他說。

他的背脊在夜晚時已經僵硬了，現在更是疼痛，而講講話可以增強他的信心。

他說：「如果你願意，就來我家住吧。很抱歉沒辦法趁起風時，揚帆讓你進來，不過我總算有個朋友作伴了。」

這時，那條大魚突然翻跳，把老人拖倒在船頭。若非及時靠好，並放出了一些釣線，他可能已經被拖進海裡了。

當釣線被拉扯時，鳥兒已經飛走了，老人來不及注意牠飛到哪裡了。他用右手小心地摸著釣線，發現手流血了。

「牠一定給什麼東西弄傷了。」他大聲地說，然後把釣線往回拉，看看能不能讓魚轉個方向。等到釣線快繃斷的時候，老人握緊不動，然後往後仰，去支撐線繩的拉力。

他說：「魚啊，你現在終於嚐到痛苦的滋味了吧？如果是的話，老天爺知道我也很痛啊。」

　　老人四處望著尋找那隻鳥，因為他渴望有牠作伴，但鳥已經飛走了。

　　老人想，你沒有停留很久，在你飛回陸地之前，途中會驚險萬分。我太笨了，好端端的怎麼會給魚一拉扯就弄傷了。可能是我只顧看著小鳥，想著牠的事，才會落到這個下場。現在我要專心工作，吃一些鮪魚，來保持體力。

　　「真希望小男孩在這裡，如果還有一些鹽就更好了。」老人大聲地說。

　　他把釣線的力量，轉移到左邊的肩膀上，小心地跪下，伸手到海水裡洗手。他浸泡了約一分鐘，看著血絲隨水漂動，小船移動時，海水規律地沖拍著他的手。

「牠游得慢多了。」他說。

老人想把手浸在鹹海水中久一點，但擔心大魚會突然翻跳起來，所以他只得站起身，振作起精神，把手朝太陽舉起來。雖然只不過是被釣線割傷手的皮肉，但卻是工作所需要用到的部位。他清楚在這場戰鬥還沒結束之前，他非常需要用到他的手。他不喜歡在還沒開始之前就掛了彩。

他的手乾了。他說：「現在，我要吃掉那條小鮪魚，我可以用魚鉤鉤過來，在這裡舒服地享用。」

他跪下來，用鉤子把鮪魚從船尾底下鉤過來，並小心避免碰到一捲捲的釣線。他依舊用左肩抵住釣線，左手和左臂支撐著，他把鮪魚從鉤子上取下來，然後把魚鉤放回原處。老人用膝蓋壓住鮪魚，用刀子將深紅色的魚肉，一條一條從魚頭到魚尾割成長條狀，從背脊骨一直割到肚子邊緣。他把魚肉切成六條，攤在船頭的木板上，然後在褲子上擦拭刀子，從尾巴處提起魚的殘骸，揮手扔到海裡去。

「看來我是吃不了整條魚了。」他說著，順手用刀子切開一條魚肉。他仍然可以感覺到釣線穩定和沉重地拉著，這時他的左手突然抽筋起來。他的左手緊抓著釣線，他不悅地看著左手。

「這是怎樣的一隻手啊，你要抽筋就抽筋吧，最好變成一隻爪子，但這對你又有什麼好處？」他說。

他心想，來吧！他沿著傾斜插入的釣線，望著深暗的海

水。把魚肉吃了吧，吃了手才有力氣。其實，也不能怪手不爭氣，因為手早就和那條魚纏鬥很久了。你可以永遠和那傢伙這麼糾纏下去。現在快把鮪魚吃了吧。

老人拿起一片魚肉，放進嘴裡，慢慢咀嚼，味道還可以。

好好嚼吧，把肉汁都吸進去，如果能加一點酸橙汁、檸檬或鹽巴，一定會更加美味，他想。

「手啊，你覺得怎麼樣？」他問那僵硬如死屍般抽筋的手。「我要替你再多吃一點。」

他把切開的另外一半魚肉也吃了。他細細咀嚼，然後把魚皮吐掉。

「手啊，你現在覺得怎樣？效果大概沒那麼快吧！」

他又拿起另外一條魚肉，放進嘴裡咀嚼。

他想：「這真是一條又肥又壯的魚。幸好釣到的是這種魚，而不是鱗鰍。鱗鰍的肉太甜，這條魚的肉一點都不甜，而且很營養。」

他想，人應該要想想現實的事，不然就沒啥意義。如果有一些鹽巴就好了。不知道太陽會不會把剩下的魚肉曬爛或曬乾。雖然我不餓，不過還是吃光比較保險。海底的那條大魚還是那麼平靜和穩定，等我把魚吃完後，就有力氣來對付牠。

「手啊，忍耐點吧，這一切都是為了你！」他說。

他想，希望把底下的那條大魚也餵得飽飽的，牠是我兄弟，但我一定要解決牠，我要保持體力才能辦得到。於是他慢條斯理、謹慎地把魚肉一條條吃完。

老人伸了伸腰，在褲子上擦了擦手。

他說：「手啊，你現在可以不用管釣線的事了，我可以先用右臂來對付牠，直到你不再作怪為止。」他將左腳踩在原先左手握住的沉甸甸的釣線，身體往後仰，支撐壓在背上的拉力。

「老天爺幫個忙吧，讓抽筋的手好起來，不知道那條大魚還會耍什麼花樣。」他說。

他想，那條魚從容不迫，按照自己的計畫進行。牠的計畫到底是什麼？而我的計畫又是什麼？我的計畫是，既然牠那麼巨大，我要想辦法來應付他。如果牠跳起來，我就能解決牠；如果牠一直潛在水底，我只好按兵不動。

他把抽筋的手在褲子上摩擦，想讓僵硬的手指靈活些，可是手掌還是無法舒展開，曬曬太陽也許會有用，他想。等生鮪魚肉消化吸收後，手也許才能張開來。萬一要用到這隻手，我會不惜代價把手張開。但我不想硬把手扳開，而要讓手自然地恢復樣子。手是因為昨晚使用過度，非得去解開釣線然後再連接起來，才會變成這個樣子的。

他放眼望過海面，發現此刻自己是多麼孤獨。他可以看到深暗海水中的折射如稜鏡一般，還有筆直往前垂入的釣絲，以及平靜中的奇異波動。

信風吹來，雲層堆得又高又厚，他往前望去，一群野鴨飛掠過水面，在天空烙下一道痕跡，消失一會兒，又再度飛回來。他知道，一個人在海上是不會感到孤單的。

他想到，有些人乘小船出海，一看不到陸地就心慌意亂，不過他知道，確實有幾個月會遇上壞天氣。但現在是颶風季節，如果颶風沒有來，那便會是全年最好的天氣。

假如在海上的話，颶風要來的前幾天，可從天空看出徵兆。他想那是在陸地上的人看不出來的，因為他們不知道要看什麼才準確，陸地會使得雲層形狀改變。不過，現在不會有颶風來就是了。

他仰望天空，白色的積雲像一層層美味的冰淇淋，再高一點的雲層，輕薄如羽毛般的卷雲，襯托著九月的晴空。

「微風，這種天氣對我比對你這條魚還有利。」他說。

老人的左手還在抽筋，不過，他試著慢慢伸展開來。

他想，我恨透抽筋，抽筋簡直是和身體作對。吃了腐壞的食物，當眾上吐下瀉固然不好意思，但獨自一個人時，抽筋更是丟自己的臉。

他想，如果小男孩在身邊，就可以幫我揉一揉，從手肘一直往下按摩。不過，它遲早不會再那麼緊繃的。

這時候，在他還沒看到水中釣線的傾斜度改變之前，他已經感覺到右手拉扯的力量有些不同了。之後他彎下身靠著釣線，左手快速地用力摩擦大腿，這時他看見傾斜的釣線緩慢地冒上來。

　　「魚上來啦。上來吧，請趕快上來吧。」老人說。

　　釣線平穩緩慢地升起，船頭前湧出一片海水，那條魚終於現身了。牠不斷往上冒，海水從牠的背脊兩側往下流。在陽光下，牠是多麼明亮耀眼，牠的頭和背部都是深紫色的，在陽光下，身體兩邊的側紋呈現出寬條紋的淡紫色。牠的長喙像棒球棍那麼長，尖得像一把利劍，牠全身都浮出了水面，然後又俐落地潛入水中，像個潛水夫一樣。老人看見牠那鐮刀似的大尾巴沒入水中，釣線也跟著飛快地滑入水裡。

　　老人說：「牠足足比這條船還要長兩呎。」釣線又穩又快地滑下去，大魚一點也沒有受到驚嚇。在釣線不被魚扯斷的情況下，老人用雙手緊握著。他知道，如果沒辦法用穩定的拉力減緩魚的速度，魚很可能會把所有的釣線都拖走，然後掙脫斷。

　　他想，牠是一條大魚，我一定得讓牠服氣。我不能讓牠知道，牠的力氣有多大，也不能讓牠知道，如果牠拚命往前游時，會有什麼狀況出現。如果我是牠，我一定會不顧一切往前衝，直到扯斷釣線為止。感謝老天爺，雖然牠比

我們高貴，而且更有能耐，但牠終究沒有我們這些捕殺者
那麼聰明。

　　老人見過許多大魚，有些重量達一千磅以上，他一生中
捕過兩條這麼重的魚，但並不是他一個人單獨辦到的。可
是現在他隻身一人，又望不到陸地，卻和一條他從沒看過
的大魚，甚至聽都沒聽過的大魚，牢牢地拴在一起。他的
左手像鷹爪般緊握著。

他想，抽筋應該會好的，一定要好起來幫助右手。有三樣東西是好兄弟：魚和我的兩隻手。抽筋一定要趕快好，不然左手就好像廢了一樣。魚的速度又慢了下來，恢復之前的速度前進。

老人想，不知道牠為什麼要冒上來，大概是要讓我看看牠有多麼龐大吧，現在我總算知道了。真希望也能讓牠知道我是什麼樣的人，但這樣牠就會看到我抽筋的手。那還是讓牠把我想像得更偉大些吧，而我也會成為我希望的那個樣子。他想，如果我是那條魚就好了，牠所要應付的就只是我的意志力和一點聰明罷了。

老人舒適地倚靠在木板上，咬著牙忍耐著痛苦的侵襲。那條魚平穩地游著，船也在海水中緩慢移動。東方吹來一陣風，掀起一陣浪潮。中午時，老人的左手不再抽筋了。

「魚啊，對你來說這真是個壞消息。」他說。然後把墊在肩膀袋子上的釣線換個位子。

雖然舒服些，但還是痛苦，不過他不承認自己的痛苦。

「我沒有信教，但如果我能抓到這條魚，我一定會誦天主經十遍，誦聖母經十遍。如果能抓到這條魚，我一定要去考柏聖女那裡去禮拜。這是我發的願。」

他下意識地開始禱告起來，有時候太累了，竟然連祈禱文都忘掉，只好快速地唸下去，讓詞句自動反射出來。他想，聖母經比天主經好唸多了。

「萬福瑪莉亞，滿被聖寵者，主與爾皆焉。女中爾為讚美，爾胎子耶穌，並為讚美。天主聖母瑪莉亞，為我等罪人，今祈天主，及我等死後，阿門。」接著他又補充道：「萬福聖母，這條魚雖然很了不起，但祈求您賜牠死亡吧。」

當他唸完祈禱文後，感覺舒服多了，但身體還是一樣疼痛，甚至比剛才還痛。他靠在船頭的木板上，規律地活動左手的指頭。

此時雖然微風輕拂，但陽光熾熱。

「我最好還是把船尾的那條釣線重新裝上魚餌。如果這條魚要跟我耗上一整晚的話，我就得再吃一點東西。瓶裡的水快沒了，我看除了鯕鰍以外，什麼東西也抓不到了，不過如果趁新鮮吃的話，鯕鰍的味道還可以。希望今晚會有一隻飛魚跳上船來，可是我又沒有燈光引誘牠，飛魚生吃最好了，而且不需要切割開。我現在要養精蓄銳。天啊，真沒想到牠這麼大！」他說道。

「我一定要解決牠，不管牠有多麼偉大，多麼了不起。」他說。

他想，雖然這並不公平，但我要讓牠知道，人類能做什麼，人類的耐力底限在哪裡。

他說：「我告訴過小男孩，我是個怪老頭，現在該是我證明的時候了。」

他想證明這件事已經上千次了，但每次都落空，現在老人又要再證明一次。每一次都是新的開始，他在證明這件事時，不會回顧過往。

他想，希望牠睡了，這樣我也可以睡一會兒，再夢見獅子。為什麼獅子在我腦海裡徘徊不去？不要胡思亂想了，老頭，他對自己這麼說。他慢慢地靠在木板上，休息了一會兒，什麼都不想。牠正在動，你要盡量節省力氣才是。

現在已經是下午了，小船依舊緩慢平穩地移動，不過東邊的微風卻使小船受到了一點阻力，老人在波浪中微微顛簸，橫過他背部的釣線變得輕鬆平順多了。

下午，釣線一度浮上來，而魚只是在比較淺的海面繼續游。太陽斜射在老人的左臂、肩膀和背上，所以他知道魚已經轉向東北方。

他已經和那條魚打過一次照面，所以他可以想見魚在水中游動的樣子。紫色的胸鰭像翅膀似地張開，豎立著的大尾巴，劃破黑暗。老人想，不知道在深海中牠能看見什麼。牠的眼睛很大，比馬眼還要大，而馬在黑暗中能看得見。以前我在黑暗中也能看得見，當然不是全暗的狀況，不過視力好的程度幾乎和貓沒什麼兩樣。

陽光的照射再加上手指持續不斷地活動，現在他左手的抽筋已經好了，於是開始讓左手分擔更多的重量，他聳聳肩，活動一下背部的肌肉，轉移一些繩索的拉力。

　　他大聲說：「魚啊，如果你還不累，那就太神奇了。」

　　他現在很累了，也知道黑夜即將來臨，於是他盡量讓自己去想其他的事，他想到大聯盟，知道紐約洋基隊正在和底特律老虎隊進行對決。

　　今天已經是賽程的第二天了，他想，不知道誰勝誰敗。但我一定要有信心，才對得起偉大的狄馬喬。他的後腳跟長了骨刺，還是忍痛把所有的事做到盡善盡美。他自問，骨刺是什麼？我們都沒長過骨刺，骨刺痛起來會不會像後腳跟有一隻鬥雞在啄？如果是那樣，我可受不了。我也沒辦法像鬥雞一樣，被啄瞎了一隻眼睛，甚至雙眼都失明了，還能繼續戰鬥。人並不比飛禽走獸強多少，不過，我倒寧願是那隻潛在深暗海水中的怪獸。

「希望鯊魚不要來，如果鯊魚來的話，請老天爺憐憫他和我吧。」他大聲地說。

你想狄馬吉歐會守著這條魚，就像我現在和這條魚糾纏不休一樣嗎？我想他會的，甚至更久，因為他年輕力壯，而且他父親也是漁夫。但骨刺會不會讓他痛得受不了？

「不曉得，我沒長過骨刺。」他大聲地說。

太陽下山了。為了增強自己的信心，老人回想起有一次在卡薩布蘭卡的酒店裡，他和一位從西恩菲柯斯來的黑人比腕力，那傢伙是這個碼頭最魁梧強壯的人。他們兩人把手肘放在畫了粉筆線的桌子上，前臂直立，兩人的手緊緊纏握住，彼此都想把對方的手壓倒在桌面上，就這樣過了一天一夜。很多人在打賭，煤油燈下，大家進進出出，他看著黑人的胳膊、手和臉。熬了八個小時後，為了讓裁判能睡覺，每隔四個小時就換一位裁判。鮮血從他和黑人的指甲縫裡滲出，他們盯著彼此的眼睛、手和前臂。打賭的人不停地進出房間，有些人坐在靠牆的高凳子上看比賽。牆是木板釘成的，漆成明亮的藍色，燈光把他們兩人的影子投射在牆上，而黑人的影子顯得巨大無比，當微風拂過那盞燈時，影子也在牆上不斷晃動著。

　　兩人你來我往，僵持了一整夜。他們給黑人喝甜酒，還為他點菸，黑人在喝完甜酒後，使出渾身的力氣，有一次還把老人的手臂壓下去三吋。那時候他還不老，而且是拿冠軍的山帝亞哥，老人又拚命地扳了回來。雖然那個黑人很不賴，也是一流的運動員，但他有把握贏過黑人。天亮了，就在下賭注的人認為乾脆平手了事，在裁判搖頭之際，他使出所有的力氣，把黑人的手一點一點地往下壓，直到壓倒在桌面上為止。比賽是從星期天早晨開始，一直持續到星期一早上才結束，許多下賭注的人因為要到碼頭

工作搬運糖包，或是去哈瓦那煤礦公司幹活，才會要求平手了事，不然誰都想知道最後是鹿死誰手。不管怎樣，他總算在那些人上工之前，把事情做個了斷。

從那次之後，有很長一段時間，每個人都叫他「冠軍」。第二年春天，他們又重新比了一局，這次下的賭注不大，因為上次的比賽已經讓那個從西恩菲柯斯來的黑人失去信心，所以他輕而易舉地就贏了。之後，他又比賽過幾次，後來就不再和人較勁了。他深信，只要他願意，他可以戰勝任何人。但他覺得太常用右手比腕力，對捕魚不太好，他也曾想過用左手練習比腕力，可是左手老像個叛逆者，不聽使喚，所以他就不再信任左手了。

他想，陽光應該把那隻手烤透了吧，除非晚上變得很冷，不然應該不會再抽筋了。不知道今晚會發生什麼事！

一架飛往邁阿密的飛機從頭頂上掠過，他看見飛機的影子把飛魚群嚇得驚慌亂竄。

「有這麼多飛魚，附近一定有鯕鰍。」他說著，身體仰靠在釣線上，看能不能把釣線拉過來一點。可是他辦不到，釣線仍繃得緊緊的，水珠不停地抖動。小船緩慢往前移動，他望著飛機遠去，直到消失在天際。

他想，坐在飛機上一定很奇妙，不知道從那麼高的地方往下看海，會是什麼樣子？如果飛得不高的話，應該可以看到這條魚，我倒希望能夠在兩百噚的高空中慢慢飛，從上面看看這條魚的樣子。以前在捕龜船上，坐在桅杆頂端的橫木上，即使是那種高度，視野都可以開闊許多。從那個高度看鱙鰍，顏色變得更青綠，牠們身上的條紋和紫斑更為明顯，而且可以看到牠們整群游動。為什麼在黑潮中游得很快的魚，背脊都呈紫色，或是通常都有紫色的條紋或斑點？鱙鰍看起來是青綠色，實際上卻是金黃色的，但當牠們餓了想吃東西時，身體兩側就會出現像馬林魚一樣紫色的條紋。難道是因為憤怒或速度太快，才會顯現出紫色的條紋？

　　在天還沒黑之前，老人的船經過了像小島般的一大叢馬尾藻，藻叢在輕波中漂動搖曳，好像海洋正躲在一條黃色的毯子下，和什麼東西在做愛似的。此時他的細釣線已經釣到一隻鱙鰍了，牠躍到空中，老人看到了在夕陽餘暉下映照著的純金色，在空中瘋狂地扭動掙扎。鱙鰍因為害怕，就像江湖賣藝的人施展絕活一樣他跳來跳去。老人走到船尾，彎下腰，右手和手臂握住粗釣繩，用左手把鱙鰍往上拉，每拉上一點，就用赤裸的左腳踩住拖過來的釣繩。鱙鰍被拉上船尾時，左右亂竄地絕望掙扎著。老人探出船身，把這條金光閃閃、身帶紫斑的魚，提上船尾。快速銜著魚鉤的下顎仍痙攣似地張合，扁長的身體、頭和尾巴，死命地拍打著船板，直到老人用棍棒敲打牠金光閃閃的頭，才顫抖了一下，便一動也不動了。

老人從魚鉤取下魚，再裝上另外一條沙丁魚餌，然後把釣線拋到海裡。他慢慢走向船頭，把左手洗乾淨，在褲管上擦乾，接著把沉重的釣繩從右手換到左手，再把右手伸到海裡洗乾淨。他望著夕陽沉入海中，然後看著傾斜插入海水的釣線。

　　「牠一點都沒改變。」他說。不過，看著流過手中的海水，他注意到牠顯然是減慢速度了。

　　老人說：「我要把兩支槳交叉綁在船尾，這樣就可以減緩牠在夜間游動的速度。牠和我一樣，都是個夜貓子。」

　　他想，等晚一點再剖鯕鰍，這樣可以保存魚肉中的血。等一下我可以一邊綁槳減緩魚的速度，一邊殺魚。在太陽下山前，最好不要驚動那條魚，讓牠保持平靜。因為對所有的魚來說，日落時分都是最難熬的時間。

　　老人把手舉起讓風吹乾，然後抓緊釣線，盡可能讓身體舒服些。他任憑自己靠在船板上，這樣一來，船就可以產

生比老人自己製造的阻力還要大。

他想，我已經慢慢學會要怎麼來對付牠了。無論如何，至少這部分是學會了。再來，牠上鉤了之後都還沒進食過，牠這麼龐大，一定需要更多的食物才夠。我已經吃了一條鰹魚了，明天再把「金色的」鬼鰍給吃了。我把牠剖開洗乾淨後，或許就應該吃一點。鬼鰍比鰹魚難吃多了，但沒有一件事是容易的，總是要去克服。

他大聲問道：「魚啊，你覺得怎麼樣？我覺得不錯，左手好多了，食物也夠吃一天一夜。魚啊，用力拖船吧。」

他並不是真的覺得很舒服，因為釣線橫跨在他背部所造成的疼痛，已經使他麻木了，這讓他開始擔心。不過他想，比這個還要慘的情況我也有過，現在只不過是手割破了一點。手的抽筋好了，腿也沒事，食物補給方面又比牠佔上風。

現在已經一片漆黑，九月時，只要太陽一下山，天就暗得很快。老人躺在船頭破舊的木板上，好好地休息。第一群星星出現了。他叫不出獵戶座「參宿七」的名字，但一看到它，就知道其他的星星很快就會出現，他就可以有這些遙遠的朋友作伴了。

　　「那條魚也是我的朋友，我沒見過、也沒聽過這麼大的一條魚，但我卻一定要把牠殺死，真高興人不用去捕殺星星。」他大聲地說。

　　試想，如果人每天都要想法子要去殺月亮，他想，月亮一定會逃走的；但再一想，萬一人每天都想要去殺太陽，那又會是什麼情況？他想，我們生下來的運氣就很好。

　　接著，老人為那條未進食的大魚感到難過，但即使再怎麼同情牠，還是沒有打消把牠解決掉的決心。他想，牠的肉可供給多少人？但這些人夠資格吃牠嗎？不，當然不夠資格，牠的一舉一動都是那麼尊貴，根本沒有人配吃牠。

　　他想，我實在是不瞭解這些事，但不用去殺太陽、月亮或星星，也是件好事。在海上討生活，捕殺我們的好兄弟，就已經足夠了。

　　現在，老人想，我應該想辦法讓大魚無法輕易地拖曳這條船，不過這樣有缺點，也有優點。如果綁住的雙槳產生魚拖曳時的阻力，船身便會加重，那麼我要放出很多釣線，魚就可能會跑掉；但如果船身很輕的話，又會延長彼

此雙方的痛苦，因為牠的速度快，卻無法施展開，這對我來說比較安全。不管怎樣，我要把鯕鰍切割好，以免腐壞了，然後吃一點來維持體力。

現在我要去休息個把個小時，等到感覺牠穩定了，再到船尾幹活，再決定採取什麼行動，這樣我也能看看牠有什麼動靜。把槳綁起來的確是個好主意，也是到目前為止比較保險的作法。牠仍然是一條了不起的魚，魚鉤鉤住牠的嘴角，嘴巴還可以閉得那麼緊。給魚鉤鉤住的痛楚不算什麼，飢餓的煎熬，再加上對對手一無所知，才夠牠受的。老頭，你先歇會兒，讓牠去掙扎吧，等一下再操心。

老人想大概已經休息了兩個小時，月亮仍未升起，也許要再晚一點，因此他無法估計現在的時間。其實，他並沒有真正的休息，只不過是放鬆點罷了。他的肩膀還是得忍受魚拖曳釣線的拉力。他把左手放在船頭舷上，將魚的拉力漸漸轉移到船身上。

他想，如果我能把釣線固定的話，該有多方便啊。不過這樣只要輕輕一拉，釣線就會被扯斷。我應該要用身體去緩衝釣繩的拉力，隨時準備用雙手放線。

「老頭子，你還沒睡覺。已經過了半天和一整夜，現在又是另一天了，你都還沒睡過覺。如果魚安靜又平穩的話，你就該想法子睡一下，要是不睡的話，腦筋可能就不清醒了。」他大聲說道。

他想，我的頭腦很清醒，太清醒了，清醒得像天空中的星星，它們都是我的兄弟。可是我還是該睡一會兒，星星要睡覺，月亮、太陽要睡覺，甚至海洋在風平浪靜時也會多睡幾天。

他想，記得要睡啊，強迫自己睡一覺，想個簡單可靠的方法控制住釣繩。現在他走到船尾將鯕鰍剖開。如果要睡的話，就不能把槳橫綁來產生阻力，那樣太危險了。

他告訴自己，我可以不睡覺，但這種作法太危險了。

他開始用手撐著跪下爬到船尾，並盡量小心不要驚動到那條大魚，他想，牠可能已經是半睡狀態。可是，我不能讓牠休息，一定要讓牠拖到死為止。

爬到船尾後，轉身過來，用左手拉住橫跨肩膀的釣線，右手從刀鞘拔出刀來。這時星光熠熠，他可以很清楚地看見鯕鰍。他把刀刃插進鯕鰍的頭，從船尾把牠挑出來。然後將另一隻腳踩在魚身上，一刀快速地從肛門直剖到下頜，然後用右手掏出肚腸，刳淨魚鰓。在掏腸時，他感覺魚的內臟既沉重又滑膩，魚肚裡還有兩條飛魚，堅硬又新鮮。他把牠們並排在一起，然後把內臟肚腸和魚鰓從船尾扔出去，那些東西沉下去時，在海水中拖出一道燐光。鯕鰍的肉已經冰冷，現在在星光下更呈現出難看的蒼白。老人一邊用右腳踩住魚頭，一邊剝去魚皮，然後再翻過來，剝去另外一面的魚皮，從頭到尾把魚肉割下來。

他把殘骸丟到船外，看看水中是否出現漩渦，但只看見慢慢沉下去的光影而已。老人轉過身，先將兩條飛魚塞入兩片鯕鰍魚肉裡，再把刀插回刀鞘裡，然後慢慢走向船頭。由於釣線的重量橫跨在肩膀上，壓得他的背傴僂著，右手拿著魚肉。

回到船頭，老人把兩片鯕鰍魚肉攤在木板上，再把兩條小飛魚放在旁邊。之後，他把肩上的釣線挪到一個新的位置，然後左手抓住釣線，靠在放槳的木拴上，之後倚著船邊，在水中把飛魚洗乾淨，感覺水從他手中流過的速度。由於魚皮黏到了他的手，所以手發出了燐光，他看著水流使燐光波動，速度已經緩慢許多。當他伸手在船身摩擦時，水面漂浮了萬點燐光，向船尾處慢慢漂去。

「牠不是累了，就是在休息。現在我得趕快吃了鯕鰍，休息一會兒，睡個覺。」老人說道。

星光下，夜晚寒意更重了，他把半片鯕鰍魚肉吃掉。飛魚的肚腸已經清理乾淨，頭也切掉了。

老人說：「如果能把鯕鰍煮熟來吃，該有多好，這種魚生吃真是難吃，以後出海一定要帶鹽或是酸橙。」

他想，如果我稍微用點腦筋的話，就應該在白天把海水潑到船裡曬乾，製造一點鹽出來。不過，我抓到這條鯕鰍時已將近黃昏了。不管怎麼說，都是我準備不夠周全。但我非得好好嚼一嚼，反正吃下去也不會有噁心的感覺。

雲層逐漸向東方天際聚攏，他所知道的星星也一顆顆消失了，此刻他彷彿朝著雲團的大峽谷前進，風速已減弱。

「三、四天後，天氣會變壞，今天或明天還不會變壞。老頭子，趁魚安靜穩定的時候，現在睡一下吧。」他說。

他右手緊抓釣線，大腿抵住右手，把全身的重量靠在船頭的木板上。然後他把肩上的釣線放低一點，再用左手支撐釣線。

他想，只要左手支撐著，右手就有足夠的力氣握緊。右手萬一因為睡著而鬆了，只要魚線一溜走，左手就會叫醒我。做事常用到右手，右手實在是太辛苦了。即使我能睡上二十分鐘或半小時也是不錯。老人弓著身子，用全身抵住釣線，把整個重量放在右手上，然後就這樣睡著了。

他沒有夢見獅子，卻夢到了一大群鼠海豚，延綿有八到十海哩這麼遠。那正是鼠海豚交配的季節，牠們跳躍到空中，再落入原來跳起時在水面所造成的小漩渦裡。

接著，他夢到自己躺在家裡的床上，北風冷颼颼，他冷得要命，右手也麻痺了，因為他把右手當枕頭擱在頭下。

然後他夢見長長的金黃色沙灘，第一頭獅子在黃昏時出現，接著其他的獅子也跟了過來。他把下巴靠在船頭的木板上，將船停泊在岸邊。傍晚時岸邊微風吹起，他等待著，想看看是不是還有更多的獅子，他很亢奮。

　　月亮已經升起好長一段時間，他仍熟睡著，那條大魚平穩地往前游，小船航向雲層的隧道裡。

　　他的右拳猛然打到了臉，驚醒了過來。釣線從右手迅速地溜出去，刮痛了他的手掌，左手沒有知覺，所以他盡量用右手控制住釣線，但釣線還是被拖走。最後他的左手終於抓住了釣線，然後用背緊勒著釣線，背脊和左手好像被燒傷一樣，左手因為承受了所有的重量，所以被割傷得很嚴重。老人回頭看備用的釣繩，仍毫無阻滯地滑入水裡，就在這個時候，那條大魚突然跳起來衝出水面，然後又倏地竄入水中。牠一再跳起來，雖然釣線不斷放出去，可是船仍移動得非常快，老人緊拉著釣線，釣線繃得很緊，且還再三瀕臨斷裂的地步。他被拉倒到整個身子貼在船頭，臉貼在切開的鱰鰍魚肉上，動彈不得。

他想，這就是我們期待的，所以讓我們共同來承擔吧。

牠拖走這麼多釣繩，非賠償不可，他想，一定要讓牠付出代價。

他看不見魚跳躍的樣子，只聽到海水飛濺，和魚落入水中時的噴水聲。釣線快速地滑出去，把他的手掌割得傷痕累累。他知道這遲早會發生，因此盡量讓釣線經過手上長繭的地方，以避免割傷手掌或手指。

　　如果小男孩在這裡，他可以幫我弄濕釣繩，他想。對啊，如果小男孩在這裡該有多好，如果他在身邊就好了。

　　釣繩不停地被拉出去，只是現在速度漸漸減緩，他只能讓魚將線一吋吋地拖走。現在他把頭從木板上抬起，貼在面頰上的魚肉已經壓爛了。老人先是跪著，然後再慢慢站起來，他仍繼續放線，但速度已經慢了下來。老人設法用腳去碰那捲他看不到的線繩，線還多得很，所以現在那條魚仍須拖曳著在水中產生摩擦阻力的新釣繩。

　　他想，是的，現在牠已經跳起來十多次了，背脊兩邊的氣囊充滿了空氣，所以不可能沉到深海裡，死在我無法把牠弄上來的地方。牠馬上就要開始繞圈子，到時候我要給牠一點顏色瞧瞧。不知道是什麼東西突然驚嚇到牠？難道是飢餓使牠難受嗎？或是被夜晚的什麼東西給嚇了一跳？牠也可能是突然感到害怕。可是牠一向都是這麼鎮定堅強，無所畏懼又充滿信心，這真是奇怪。

　　他說：「老頭，你應該也不要害怕，對自己要有信心。你現在雖然拉住了牠，卻無法把線收回來，不過不久牠就要開始繞圈子了。」

　　現在老人用左手和肩膀來拉住魚，彎下身子，用右手掬水，把臉上的鯕鰍碎肉洗掉，他怕那些東西會令他想吐，而嘔吐會讓他沒體力。臉洗乾淨後，他將右手伸入水裡，泡在鹽水中，直到太陽升起了第一道曙光。他想，牠朝偏

東的方向游去，表示牠已經累了，所以才順著海流前進。不久牠就會轉圈子，那時候我們的對決才要真正要開始。

老人認為他的右手已經在水裡泡得夠久了，於是把它拿出來看看。

「還不算太慘，對一個男子漢來說，這一點疼痛算不了什麼。」他說。

他小心謹慎地握著釣線，不讓新滑出去的釣繩再割傷手。他轉移身體重心，以便將手放到船另一邊的海水裡。

他對著左手說：「跟廢物比起來，你還不算一無是處。可是，有一陣子，你真讓我洩氣。」

他想，為什麼我與生俱來不是兩隻好手？也許沒有好好訓練左手，這是我的過失，但老天爺知道，它應該有很多機會學習才對。不過，左手昨晚表現得不算太差，只抽筋過一次，如果再抽筋的話，就讓釣線把它割斷好了。

他知道自己的頭腦有點不大清楚了，應該再多吃一些鯕鰍肉。但他告訴自己，不能再吃了，與其吃了嘔吐傷元氣，還不如現在輕微的頭暈。我知道吃了一定會吐，因為剛才臉還貼著鯕鰍肉，現在想起來還很噁心。我先把鯕鰍魚肉留著，在情況危急時再吃，如果壞了就丟掉。現在要靠吃東西來增加體力，已經太遲了。你真笨，他對自己說，把另外一條飛魚吃掉不就成了。

那條飛魚還乾淨、好整以暇地準備好放在那邊，他用左手拾起一片吃下去，再小心翼翼地嚼著魚刺，從頭到尾將整條魚吃光。

　　他想，飛魚應該算是最富營養的魚，至少牠能提供我所需要的體力。他想，我已經盡力而為了，讓那條魚開始轉圈子，將我們的戰鬥揭開序幕吧。

　　從他出海算起，太陽已經是第三次升起了，魚才開始轉圈子。

　　他從釣線的傾斜度，無法看出魚是否在打轉。現在還太早了，所以看不出來，他只感覺釣線的張力，稍微鬆弛了一些。他用右手輕輕地拉緊釣線，釣線又如往常一樣繃緊，但當緊繃得快要斷裂時，又開始鬆了下來。他將釣線繞過肩膀和頭，開始用雙手輪替把釣線平穩、輕輕地往回收，老人使盡全身和腿的力量，老腿和肩膀順著釣線的拉力來回擺動。

　　「牠繞了一大圈，但至少已經開始打轉了。」他說。

　　然後釣線無法再收回了，他握住釣線，看著釣線在陽光下迸出水珠來。接著，釣線飛快地脫手出去，老人跪了下來，無可奈何地望著釣線竄回黑黝黝的水裡。

「牠現在正在遠處繞圈子。」他說。他想,我要盡量抓住釣線,釣線的拉力會讓牠繞的圈子愈來愈小,或許再一個鐘頭我就能看到牠了,現在我要讓牠心服口服,然後再把牠解決掉。

但兩個小時過去了,那條魚仍不疾不徐地繞圈子,老人渾身已被汗水濕透,累得骨頭都痠痛起來了。不過,現在牠繞的圈子已經小多了,從釣線的傾斜度,他可以知道魚已經慢慢地游上來。

大約有一個小時之久,老人眼前直冒黑點,汗水浸濕了他的眼睛、眼眶和前額周圍的傷口。眼前所冒的黑點嚇不倒他,那是他用力拉扯釣線而緊張的正常現象。不過,讓他覺得煩惱的是,他已經有兩次感到頭暈目眩。

「我不能夠因為一條魚就被打敗,送掉老命。我都已經這麼漂亮地弄到手了,老天爺就請幫我再熬下去,我會唸一百遍的天主經和聖母經,只是現在我無法唸。」他說。

他想，就當我已經誦過了，我以後一定會補誦。

這時候，他忽然感覺兩隻手握住的釣線猛然間被扯動，猛烈、結實又沉重。

那條魚正用長喙撞擊釣線上的浮鉤，他想這是意料中的事，牠非得這麼做不可。但這樣會讓牠跳起來，我寧願牠現在一直繞圈子。牠一定要跳起來呼吸空氣，可是每跳一次，鉤在嘴上的裂痕就會加大，到最後會把鉤子給甩掉。

他說：「不要跳，魚啊，不要跳。」

魚又撞了浮標幾次，每撞一次，老人就得多放出一些釣線。

他想，我不能再增加牠的痛苦了，我的痛苦算不了什麼，我忍受得住，可是痛苦會逼得牠發瘋。

過了一會兒，魚不再撞擊浮標了，又開始兜圈子。老人現在開始收回釣線，但他又感到一陣暈眩，於是用左手掬起海水，從頭淋下，然後又用了一些水搓揉頸背。

他說：「我沒有抽筋，牠很快就要浮上來了，我一定可以撐得住。你一定要撐下去，這還用說嗎？」

他靠著船頭跪下來，立刻再把釣線勒在背上。牠在繞圈子的時候，我可以歇息一會兒，等到牠冒上來時，再來好好對付牠，老人就這麼決定了。

靠在船頭休息，不去管那根釣線，任那條魚去繞圈子，是多麼愜意的事。但釣線的張力告訴他，那條魚靠近了小船。他站起身，開始將能夠收回的釣線收了回來。

他想，我從來沒這麼累過。現在已經吹起信風了，趁風吹起時，將牠拖上來，我需要那陣風。

「在牠繞下一圈時，我可以休息一下，我已經感到舒服多了。等牠再繞兩、三圈後，我就可以逮到牠。」他說。

他的草帽溜到腦後，當魚轉彎時，他就被拖倒在船頭。

魚啊，你開始轉吧，等你轉完圈子，我就可以逮住你。

海水已經漲得很高了，但今天是微風吹拂的好天氣，我得靠這陣風帶我回家。

「只要朝西南方向划就可以，那就不會迷失在海洋裡，何況我住的村落是一座狹長的島嶼。」他說。

那條魚繞第三圈時，老人才頭一次看到牠。

起先老人看到一抹黑影，花了好久的時間從船底掠過，他簡直無法相信牠有那麼長。

「不，牠不可能有那麼大。」他說。

但牠的確就是那麼大。繞完一圈後，牠浮出水面，離老人大約有三十碼遠，他看見牠的尾巴露出水面，比大鐮刀的刀鋒還要高，在深藍色的水中呈現淡紫色。魚在水面下游動，尾巴往後傾斜，老人可以看見牠龐大的身軀和鑲在身上的紫色條紋。牠的背鰭下垂，巨大的胸鰭向外展開。

魚在轉這一圈時，老人看見了牠的眼睛，還有兩條灰色的魚在牠附近游來游去。那兩條魚時而緊靠著牠，時而游到別處，有時又自由自在地在牠的身影處游動。那兩條魚都超過三呎長，游得快時像鰻魚似地猛烈搖擺。

老人汗流浹背，但並不是因為太陽曬的關係。大魚從容平穩地轉圈子，每轉一圈，他就趕緊收回一些釣線。他想只要牠再繞兩圈，他就有機會把魚叉射到牠身上。

我得想法子讓牠再靠近些，他想。我不要刺牠的頭，一定要直刺牠的心臟。

「老頭子，你要沉著堅強。」他自語道。

在繞下一圈時，魚的背脊露出水面，但離船還是遠了些。再轉下一圈時，仍然太遠，但牠已經高高冒出海面。老人想，只要再收回一些釣線，就可以把牠拖到船邊了。

魚叉老早就準備好了，綁在魚叉上的一捆細繩，放在圓形的籃子裡，而繩子的另一端緊繫在船頭的木樁上。

　　現在魚繞著圈子游近小船，從容優雅，只見牠擺動的大尾巴。老人使盡力氣把牠拖近一點，魚往他這邊斜側了一下身，不到一會兒，又擺正開始轉另一圈。

　　老人說：「我終於拖動牠了，我拖動牠了。」

　　這時他又感到一陣暈眩，但仍死命地拉住那條魚。他想，我終於拉動牠了，也許這次我就能把牠拖過來。他想著：手，拉啊！腳，站穩啊！頭腦呀，為了我，你一定要保持清醒啊！這一次我一定要把牠拖過來。

在魚還沒靠近船身時，老人就使出全力拚命拉，魚於是掉轉身子，筆直地游開。

老人說：「魚啊，魚，反正你遲早要死，難道也要我陪你一起死嗎？」

他想，這樣下去是沒有結果的。他口渴得已經講不出話來，但現在又無法伸手拿水來喝。他想，這次一定要把牠拖過來，如果牠再多轉幾圈，我可能就沒辦法每次都保持良好的狀況。他告訴自己，你可以的，你一直都很行的。

牠在轉下一圈時，他差一點就把牠給拖過來，可是牠又挺直身子慢慢游開。

老人心想，魚啊，你簡直是要我的命啊！但你有權利這麼做的，兄弟。我這輩子還沒見過比你更大、更漂亮、更鎮定、更高貴的魚了。過來殺死我好了，不管誰殺死誰，我都不在乎。

他想，現在你腦筋有點糊塗了，你要保持頭腦清醒。保持頭腦清醒，像個男子漢或像魚那樣咬緊牙根，他想。

「腦子，清醒！清醒！」老人用幾乎聽不見的聲音說。

那條魚又照老樣子轉了兩圈。

他想，我實在搞不懂，牠每轉一圈，他就覺得自己快要暈厥過去。我已經糊塗了，我要再試一次。

他又試了一次，當他把魚拖轉過來時，覺得自己快暈過去了。而魚又挺直身子，在空中搖著大尾巴，慢慢游開。

　　我一定要再試一次，老人對自己發誓，雖然他的手已經開始無力，視線也模糊了。

　　他又試了一次，結果仍然一樣。所以他想，都還沒開始他就快昏厥過去，我非得再試一次不可。

　　他忍住疼痛，使盡所有的力量和久違的自尊，和魚的痛苦相對抗。魚終於游到了船邊，在他身旁慢慢地游來游去。魚的尖嘴幾乎要碰到船板，牠開始沿著船邊游，又長、又高、又寬，銀色的身軀鑲著紫色的條紋，在海水中無止盡地伸展開來。

老人放下釣線，用腳踩住，然後盡可能地舉起魚叉，使出渾身的力氣，將魚叉刺入魚巨大胸鰭的後方兩側。那條魚的胸鰭高高地挺立在半空中，幾乎和人的胸部齊高，他能感覺出鐵叉已經穿進牠的身體。於是他握緊魚叉，再刺深一點，把全身的重量都壓進去。

　　隨後那條魚活蹦亂跳，死亡已經降臨在牠身上。牠高高地躍出水面，展露牠令人讚嘆的長度、寬度、力量和眩人的美麗。牠像是懸掛在老人小船的上空，然後又重重地跌入海裡，水花濺到了老人和小船。

　　老人覺得頭暈目眩，但還是弄好魚叉的繩索，讓繩索慢慢滑過他皮開肉綻的手。當視線清楚時，他看見魚翻著銀色的肚皮，魚叉的柄部和魚的肩部形成了一個角度。從心臟噴出的血染紅了海水，開始時是在大約一英哩深處，像

在深藍色的水裡形成黑色的沙洲一般，然後又像雲彩般擴散開來。魚閃耀著銀白色，靜止不動地隨著海水浮沉。

老人用微弱的目光，用力地瞧了一眼，然後把魚叉上的繩索，在船頭的木樁上繞了兩圈，隨後把頭靠在手上。

他對著船頭板說道：「頭腦要保持清醒，現在已經把這條魚解決了，牠是我兄弟。雖然我是個疲倦的老頭，但現在我還得做辛苦的善後工作。」

他想，現在我要準備繩套和繩子，把魚綁在船邊。雖然只有我和這條大魚，但如果把牠裝上船，那麼小船會浸滿了水，就算一瓢瓢把水汲出，小船也是撐不住。我要打點好一切，把牠拖過來綁好，然後豎好桅杆，揚起風帆啟程回航。

他開始把魚拖過來靠近船邊，用繩子穿過魚鰓，再從嘴裡拉出，把牠的頭緊綁在船頭上。老人想，我要看看牠、摸摸牠，感覺牠的存在。他想，牠是我的財產，但這不是我要感受牠的原因。當我第二次把魚叉刺入牠的身體時，他想，我已感受到牠的心跳。現在他把牠拖過來，緊緊捆住，將繩套套住牠的尾巴，然後另外一個繩套套在牠身體的中間，綁在小船上。

「快去幹活吧，老頭子。」他說道，並喝了一小口水。「雖然戰鬥已經結束，但還有很多辛苦的工作要做。」

他抬頭望望天空，然後又看看他的魚。他仔細看著太陽，他想，現在才過正午不久，信風已經吹起。此時亂成一團的釣線已經無關緊要了，等回家後，我和小男孩可以再把這些線編結起來。

「來吧，魚。」他說。可是魚並沒有過來，而是躺在海水上顛簸著，老人只好把小船划移向魚。

當他靠近魚，把魚頭靠近船頭時，難以置信這條魚有這麼大。他把繫在魚叉上的繩子從木樁上解開，穿進魚鰓，從嘴巴拉出，在尖嘴上繞一圈，再從另一邊的魚鰓穿出去，在尖嘴上又再繞一圈，再將兩邊的繩子打個結，緊緊地綁在船頭的木樁上。接著他把多餘的繩子切斷，走到船尾，把魚的尾巴也套住。魚已經由原來的紫色和銀色，變成全然的銀色，牠的條紋和尾巴呈現出蒼白的淺紫色，那

些條紋比人的手指全部張開還要寬。魚眼睛看起來就像潛望鏡兩邊的鏡面，或是像禮拜行進中的聖徒，分得很開。

「要解決牠只有這個辦法。」老人說。喝過水後，他覺得舒服多了，他的頭腦很清醒，確定自己不會再暈眩。他想，看樣子這條魚可能有一千五百磅，甚至更重。剖開處理後，起碼還有三分之二的魚肉，一磅三毛錢如何？

他說：「我需要用鉛筆算一下，我的頭腦還沒那麼清楚。但我相信，連偉大的狄馬喬也會為我今天的勝利感到驕傲。雖然我沒有長過骨刺，但手和背部的疼痛也夠受的了。」老人想，不知道骨刺長得怎樣，也許我們有長過，只是不知道那是骨刺罷了。

他把魚緊綁在船頭船尾和中央坐板的位置，這條魚實在是太大了，所以就像是拖了一艘更大的小船在旁一樣。他割下一段繩子，把魚的下巴和尖嘴綁起來，以免嘴巴張開，這樣航行才能盡量不受阻礙。接著他豎起桅杆，用魚叉的桿子和帆下的木桁，升起滿是補釘的風帆。船開始移動，老人半躺在船尾，朝西南方航行。

他不需要靠指南針來得知西南方的方位，只要從信風和風帆的吹動情形就能知道了。我最好放一根短釣線到海裡，弄點東西來吃，並喝點東西保持水分。可是他找不到鉤子，沙丁魚餌也腐壞了。於是他用魚叉撈起一把馬尾藻，把躲在裡面的小蝦抖落在船板上。十多隻小蝦子在上面跳來跳去，活像跳蚤似的。老人用拇指和食指把牠們的頭拔掉，連尾帶殼吃下去。蝦子雖小，但他知道牠們既富營養，味道又鮮美。

老人的瓶子裡還剩兩口水就沒了，吃完小蝦子後，他喝了半口水。雖然小船挺累贅的，但航行很順利。他把舵柄夾在腋窩裡，他可以看到那條魚，而唯有看著他的手，去感覺背部抵住船尾的感覺，他才能確定這一切千真萬確發生過，而不是一場夢。他一度覺得自己快完蛋了，但又想這大概只是一場夢吧。然後當他看到魚躍出水面，在牠落下海水之前，在半空中呈現靜止狀態，他感到不可思議。現在他能看得和往常一樣清楚，但剛剛是看不清楚的。

而現在他可以確定這條魚確實存在了，他的手和背都能

證明這不是在做夢。他想，手會很快痊癒，血流乾淨後，鹽水會治療好這些傷口，海灣中的深暗色海水真是一帖萬靈藥。我所要做的，就是保持頭腦清醒，我的手可說是鞠躬盡瘁了，航行也很順利。牠的嘴巴緊閉，尾巴直豎著上下起伏，我們像親兄弟一般並肩而行。然後他腦筋又開始有點不清楚了，他想，究竟是牠拖著我走？還是我拖著牠走？如果是我把牠拖在後面，當然不容置疑；如果魚顏面盡失地在我的小船上，那也毫無疑問，可是我們卻是綁在一起、並肩而行啊。老人想，假如這樣能讓牠高興的話，就算是牠拖著我走吧。牠從未傷害過我，而我只是比牠善用計謀罷了。

他們航行地很順利，老人把手浸泡在海水裡，以保持頭腦清醒。雲層堆積得很高，還形成了許多卷雲，老人知道微風會整晚吹個不停。他不時望著魚，以確定真有那麼一回事。一小時後，第一條鯊魚開始襲擊他。

鯊魚的出現並非偶然，魚的暗色血水擴散到一哩深的海水，鯊魚便從海水深處竄上來。鯊魚竄得很快，衝破藍色的海水，出現在陽光下。然後又鑽進海裡，循著血腥味，順著船和魚被拖走的路線游過來。

有時候牠會聞不到血腥味，不過很快又會嗅出來，或僅憑一絲微弱的氣味，便飛快地沿著留下的痕跡游過來。這是一條巨大的灰鯖鯊，是海中游得最快的魚，除了下顎外，外型很漂亮，背脊像旗魚一樣藍，肚子呈銀色，皮膚

光滑漂亮；除了巨大的下顎外，其他的樣子都長得像旗魚。游得快時，下顎緊閉，高聳的背鰭像一把刀子劃過水面，毫不擺動。在牠緊閉的嘴裡，八排牙齒全向內傾斜，牠的牙齒不像大多數鯊魚一樣呈三角形，牠們蜷曲起來像爪子般的牙齒，就而像人類的手指一樣，而且有老人的手指那麼長；兩側的牙齒，有如剃刀般尖銳。這種魚天生下來就可以吞食海裡所有的魚，他們游得那麼快，體型健壯，全身武裝，所向無敵。現在，牠嗅到了新鮮的血腥味，藍色的背鰭劃過水面游了過來。

　　老人看見牠游過來時，就知道這是一條天不怕地不怕、為所欲為的鯊魚。他緊盯著鯊魚，準備好魚叉，將繩索綁緊。由於割了一段繩索綁大魚，所以剩下的繩子很短。

　　現在老人的頭腦很清醒，雖然意志堅定，但是希望仍然甚為渺茫。他想，美好的事情難以長久。他看見鯊魚游近時，看了大魚一眼。他想，也許這根本就是一場夢吧。我

沒有辦法阻止牠來攻擊我，但我或許可以制伏他。大牙齒的，老人想，他媽的真是倒楣。

　　鯊魚飛快地逼近船尾，當牠襲擊大魚時，老人看到牠張大的嘴巴和古怪的眼睛，還聽見牠咬下魚尾肉，牙齒喀擦的聲響。鯊魚的頭露出海面，背脊也挺出水面。老人把魚叉朝牠橫過兩眼和直劃鼻子的兩條線所形成的交叉點刺進時，他聽到了大魚皮綻肉開的聲音。其實，根本就沒有所謂的兩條線，只有那顆又重又尖的藍色頭顱和大眼睛，還有咯咯作響、吞得下一切的大嘴巴。那個交叉點是牠頭腦的位置，老人就往那裡刺下去。他使盡所有的力氣，用沾

滿鮮血的手把魚叉擲了出去。當他擲出魚叉時，心中並不抱任何希望，但卻充滿了決心和全然的敵意。

　　鯊魚翻了個身，老人從牠的眼神知道牠快死了。接著牠再翻滾了一圈，被繩子纏了兩圈，老人確定牠是死定了。然而鯊魚不肯承認這個事實，牠翻著肚皮，尾巴撲打著水面，兩顎格格作響，像快艇似地掙扎游動。牠的尾巴攪動起白色的水花，身體有四分之三浮出海面，繩子繃得很緊，顫抖了一下，然後突然間斷掉。老人注視著鯊魚動也不動地浮在海面上，過了一會兒，牠便慢慢地沉下去了。

　　老人大聲地說：「牠大概吃掉了四十磅的肉。」他想，牠也把僅有的魚叉和繩索都帶走了。現在我的魚又流著血，一定會引來其他的鯊魚。

那條魚殘缺不全，老人不忍再看牠一眼。他覺得剛才鯊魚攻擊的不是這條魚，而是自己。

他想，我已經把攻擊大魚的鯊魚殺掉了。老天爺知道我看過很多大魚，但這隻鯊魚是我見過最大的「大牙齒」。

他想，美好的事物總是那麼短暫。現在真希望這一切都是夢，但願我根本就沒有釣到這條大魚，只不過是獨自一人躺在床上看報紙罷了。

他說：「人不是為失敗而生。人可以被摧毀，卻不能被擊敗。」他想，殺了大魚，我感到很難過。現在艱難的時刻又來了，而我連一支魚叉都沒有。「大牙齒」雖然殘酷、神勇、強壯、聰明，但我還比牠聰明些。不，可以不是這樣，他想，大概只是因為我的武器比牠還要銳利。

「別再想了，老頭子，還是順著航線往前吧，一切船到橋頭自然直。」他大聲地說。

不過我非得好好想想不可。他想，因為我除了胡思亂想和棒球，什麼也不剩了。不知道偉大的狄馬喬喜不喜歡我擊中魚頭的樣子？其實這也沒什麼了不起。他想，誰都做得到。你想我雙手的疼痛和骨刺是不是一樣痛？這我無從得知。我的腳後跟好像沒出過什麼毛病，除了有一次在游泳時被黃貂魚的刺螫了一下，小腿頓時麻痺，痛楚難忍。

他說：「想點愉快的事吧，老頭子。現在每過一分鐘，就離家更近了。少了四十磅的重量，航行起來輕快多了。」

船航行至海潮中會發生什麼狀況，他清楚得很，但他現在無法預作準備。

「有辦法了，我可以把刀子綁在槳柄上。」他大聲說。

於是，他把舵夾在腋窩下，用腳踩住帆索。

他說：「現在我雖然是個老頭，但可不是手無寸鐵。」

微風涼爽地吹著，航行也很順利。老人望著魚的前半部，又尋回了一線希望。

他想，心中不存希望的人太愚蠢了，而且他覺得這是一種罪惡。問題已經夠多了，還是不要去想罪惡吧，這我又不懂。

我不懂罪惡，也不確定是否相信罪惡。也許殺魚是罪惡，就算是為了討生活、供魚肉給人吃，也是有罪。這樣說來，每件事都有罪。不要去想這些了，現在談這個太遲了，就讓吃牠的人去想好了，這些人要付出代價。你生下來就是要當漁夫，就像大魚生下來就是魚一樣，或是像桑彼得羅或偉大狄馬喬的父親一樣，生下來就是要當漁夫。

但是，他喜歡思索經歷過的事。他沒有書報可以看，沒有收音機可以聽，便繼續思考罪惡這件事。他想，你並不僅僅是為了生存或出售魚肉，才殺死那條魚的。你殺死牠，是因為你是漁夫，你有自尊心。牠生前時，你很愛牠，死後你依然如此。如果愛牠，殺了牠就不算是罪惡，還是罪孽會更深重？

他大聲說道：「老頭子，你想太多了。」

他想，但你殺死「惡魔」時，感覺就很痛快。鯊魚也和你一樣，靠捕食魚為生。但牠不像有些鯊魚，會吃腐爛的食物，或是有什麼就吃什麼。牠美麗又高貴，無所畏懼。

老人高聲說：「我殺牠是為了自衛，而且方法高明。」

此外，他想，一物剋一物，只是方法不同罷了。魚能致我於死地，正如魚能養活我一樣。他想，是那小男孩養活我的，我還是不要自欺欺人才好。

他倚靠著船邊，從鯊魚咬過的地方撕下一片魚肉，放進嘴裡咀嚼，品嚐肉質的鮮美。魚肉結實又多汁，像一般的肉一樣，但並不是鮮紅色的。還有，肉裡沒有筋，他知道這在市場上可以賣到最好的價錢。然而，不讓血腥味飄到海水裡是不可能的，老人知道，艱難的時刻就要來臨。

微風不斷吹著，風略微吹向東北方，他知道這表示風不會減弱。老人朝前望去，看不見帆影，也見不著半艘船，更不用說看到船上所冒出的煙了。只有飛魚從船頭向兩側掠過，還有一簇簇黃色的馬尾藻。連一隻鳥也沒看見。

他已經航行兩個小時了。他靠在船尾休息，有時候從馬林魚身上撕下肉，放在嘴裡咀嚼，盡量藉著休息來養精蓄銳。這時候，他又看到了兩條鯊魚中的第一條。

「哎呀。」他喊道，這個叫聲並無法傳達他的感受。也許當一個人的手被釘子穿過，釘在木板上時，會不由自主

95

地發出這種聲音。

「虎鯊。」他大聲說。這時他看到第二隻鰭尾隨著第一隻。從棕色三角形的背鰭和尾巴搖擺的動作，他可以斷定這兩條鯊魚是有鏟形鼻頭的虎鯊。牠們嗅到了血腥味，非常亢奮，餓昏了頭，到處尋覓氣味，現在越來越接近了。

老人把帆鎖拴牢，舵柄綁緊，再把綁著刀子的槳拿起來。他盡可能輕輕地舉起槳，因為手很痛，不聽指揮。他把手張開來又握緊，活動一下筋骨。然後握緊手，以利於忍住疼痛。他毫不畏縮地注視鯊魚的來到。現在他能看到牠們寬闊、扁平如鏟子尖端的頭，以及白色尖尖的胸鰭。牠們是令人厭惡的鯊魚，發出一股惡臭，吃腐爛的食物，有如殺手一般殘酷。肚子餓的時候，連槳和船舵都會被咬一口。這種鯊魚會趁海龜在海面上熟睡時，咬掉海龜的腳和蹼。只要餓了，牠們也會攻擊水中的人類，就算人的身上沒有沾上魚的血腥味或黏液，也會遭到襲擊。

老人說：「喂！虎鯊，過來吧，虎鯊。」

牠們來了。不過，牠們來的方式和先前的灰鯖鯊不同。其中一條轉了一圈，便游到船下，不見蹤影，老人感到小船一陣晃動，原來牠去拉扯那條大魚。另外一條睜著黃色的眼睛，直瞪著老人，半開著嘴巴，然後迅速地朝大魚原先的傷口咬了下去。在那條鯊魚棕色的頭頂和大腦及脊髓相接的背脊，有一條很清楚的線。老人用綁在槳上的刀子，朝兩條線的交會點刺過去，抽回來後，又刺向牠貓似的黃眼睛。最後鯊魚鬆了口，臨死前還硬把嘴裡的魚肉吞下去。

小船依舊搖晃得很厲害，另外一條鯊魚正在啖食大魚。老人鬆開帆索，讓船斜向一邊，讓船底下的鯊魚暴露出來。老人一看到鯊魚，便傾身往牠身上刺過去，他只刺到鯊魚的肉，因為皮太厚了，要勉強把刀子刺進去很困難。老人這麼用力一下，不但手痛了起來，也傷到了肩膀。鯊

魚快速地把頭露出水面，當牠的鼻子露出水面、靠向大魚時，老人再度準確地擊中牠扁平頭部的交叉點。老人抽出刀子，往同樣的地方再刺進去。但牠仍用上下顎咬住大魚不放，老人於是往牠的左眼刺下去，鯊魚還是緊咬住大魚不鬆開。

「你還不放？」老人說。然後把刀戳入脊椎骨與大腦中間，這一次很容易就刺進去了，他感覺到鯊魚的軟骨斷掉了。老人把槳反過來，用刀撬開牠的上下顎，在牠嘴裡翻攪一通，鯊魚便鬆口了。他說：「滾開吧，虎鯊。沉到一哩深，去找你的朋友吧，說不定還是你媽媽。」

老人將刀刃擦拭乾淨，放下槳，之後找到帆索，揚起風帆，小船又朝正確的航線駛去。

老人大聲說道：「那些鯊魚一定已經吃掉了四分之一了，而且都是上好的魚肉。真希望這根本就是一場夢，我也沒釣到這條魚。我感到太抱歉了，魚啊，一切都錯了。」他不再說話，也不願再看魚一眼。魚的血已經流光，被海水沖刷乾淨，牠的顏色看起來如鏡子的銀白色，條紋依然可見。

老人說：「魚啊，我不應該出海這麼遠。對你、對我，都沒有好處，魚啊，真是對不起。」

老人自言自語了一陣，看看綁在刀上的繩子是不是斷了。先把你的手弄好，因為還有更多的鯊魚馬上要來了。

「希望有塊石頭可以用來磨刀子，我應該帶塊石頭來的。」老人檢查過綁在槳柄上的繩子後說道。他想，你應該要帶的東西可多著了，可是老頭子，你偏偏什麼都沒帶。現在不是在想你缺什麼東西的時候，而是想該怎樣利用現有的東西。

「你替我出了不少好主意，可是，我已經厭煩了。」他大聲說。

小船繼續往前航行，老人把槳柄夾在腋下，雙手浸泡在海水裡。

「不知道最後那條鯊魚吃掉了多少肉，小船輕多了。」他說。他不願去想被鯊魚扯得殘缺不全的魚肚子。他知道，鯊魚每次猛扯，就會撕下一大片魚肉，現在那條鯊魚替所有的鯊魚開了一條通道，猶如在海中開了一條大道。

他想，這條大魚足足可吃一個冬天。不要再想這件事了，只要歇一會兒，把手弄好，才能保護剩下的魚肉。海水的血腥味那麼濃，我手上的血算不了什麼，更何況手上的血也不多，雖然沒什麼，但流血可以讓手不再抽筋。

現在我能想什麼？他想，什麼事都不要想，什麼事都不該想，準備等下一群鯊魚來就夠了。他想，真希望這是一場夢，但誰知道？也許會有好的結局也說不定。

接著來的是一隻落單的鏟鼻鯊，牠游過來的模樣，就像一隻進槽吃飼料的豬。如果豬的嘴巴有牠那麼大的話，你就可以把頭伸進去了。老人讓牠去咬大魚，然後用綁在槳上的刀子，刺進牠的腦袋。但當鯊魚猛然往後退時，刀子突然斷成兩截。

當大鯊魚緩緩沉入海水時，老人連看都不看一眼，只管掌舵。鯊魚起先還很大，然後愈沉愈小，最後只剩一丁點了。這種景象原本一直很令老人著迷，但他現在連看都不看。

「我現在還有魚鉤，但這沒有用。我還剩兩把槳、一把舵柄和一根短棍。」他說。

這一回，牠們可把我打敗了。他想，我太老了，沒辦法把鯊魚群一一打死，不過，只要我手上還有槳、舵柄和短棍，我就要奮戰到底。

老人又把手浸泡在水中，天色已經接近傍晚，除了海和天之外，什麼也看不到，天空中的風比先前還要大得多，他希望不久就可以看到陸地。

他說：「老頭子，你累了，你打從心底感到疲倦了。」

太陽剛西下，鯊魚又來攻擊老人。

他看見兩尾棕色的鰭，沿著大魚在水中所形成的路徑游來。牠們不是循著血腥味，而是肩並肩地朝小船游過來。

老人把舵拴緊，綁牢帆索，從船尾下摸出一根短木棍，那原本是斷槳鋸成的舵把，大約有兩呎半長。由於棍子上有一個把手，所以單手拿比較好，老人右手緊緊握住，曲

著手指，緊盯著游過來的鯊魚，這兩條都是虎鯊。

他想，我得等第一條鯊魚緊咬住魚肉時，朝牠的鼻尖或腦袋的正中央直敲下去。

兩條鯊魚一起靠近，他看見離他比較近的那條鯊魚張開大嘴巴，埋入大魚銀色的身軀。老人高舉短棍，重重地朝鯊魚寬闊的頭頂劈下去。短棍擊下時，他感覺像是擊在堅硬的橡皮上，但他也感覺是敲在硬骨頭上。當鯊魚放開大魚滑下來時，他又對準牠的鼻尖，狠狠敲了一記。

另外一條鯊魚咬了一口，又游開，現在又張著大嘴游了過來。當牠撞上大魚，一口咬下，再合上嘴巴時，他看到一塊塊白色的魚肉從嘴角掉落。他只往牠的頭敲下去，鯊魚望著他，用力撕下魚肉。當牠把肉吞下游開時，老人再度揮棒打牠，但只打到厚如硬橡皮的東西上。

「來吧，虎鯊，再來吧。」老人說。

鯊魚又衝了過來，當牠閉上嘴巴時，他盡可能舉高木棍，再狠狠地敲了一下。這一次好像打中了頭骨，因此再朝同一地方擊下去。鯊魚有氣無力地撕下一塊魚肉，然後從大魚身上滑了下去。

老人等著牠再回來，但鯊魚卻沒出現。過了一會兒，老人看見一條鯊魚在海面上轉圈子，除此之外，沒有看見其他的鯊魚。

他想，要把牠們收拾掉是沒指望了。想當年我是能辦到的，但現在至少牠們已經被我傷得很嚴重，牠們也不會好受的。如果可以用雙手握棍子打，說不定已經解決第一條鯊魚了。他想，就算是現在，我也還有這個能耐。

他不願意去看大魚一眼，他知道牠已經被毀了一半。老人在和兩條鯊魚搏鬥時，太陽已經落下。

他說：「天很快就黑了，沒多久我就會看到哈瓦那的燈火。如果我太偏東的話，就會看到新海灘上的燈光。」

他想，現在離岸不會太遠了。希望不要有人為我操心，當然，只有小男孩會為我擔心，但我知道他對我有信心。很多老漁夫也會擔心，還有其他人也會。他想，我住在一個和善的小鎮上。

魚毀傷得太厲害了，他已經無法和牠講話了。這時，他頭腦閃過一個念頭。

「你這半條魚啊，你原本是一條完整的魚。很抱歉我出海太遠，把我們兩個都毀了，但你我共同殺死、打傷了很

多條鯊魚，老魚啊，你殺死過多少魚？你嘴上的長喙沒白長啊。」他說。

他喜歡去想像如果那條大魚可以自由自在地游動，牠會怎樣對付鯊魚。我應該把大魚的尖嘴砍下來去和鯊魚搏鬥。可是船上沒有斧頭，也沒有刀子。

我要是有斧頭和刀子，就可以把尖嘴綁在槳柄上，那將會是多麼犀利的武器啊。這樣我們就可以並肩作戰了。如果鯊魚夜晚來攻擊，你現在會怎麼辦？你能怎麼辦？

「和牠們搏鬥，我會和牠們奮戰到死為止。」他說。

天色已經暗下來了，看不見星光也看不見燈火，只有風吹拂著和扯緊的帆。老人覺得搞不好已經是亡魂了，他合著雙手，感覺一下雙掌，手掌沒有死，只要張合一下手掌，就可以從中感受到生命的痛楚。他把背靠在船尾，知道自己還沒死，他背上的疼痛這樣告訴他。

他心想，我發願如果捕到這條魚，就要念祈禱文，但我

現在累得念不出來。我還是把布袋拿來，蓋在肩膀上吧。

他躺在船尾，掌著舵，凝望天空的光影。老人想，我只剩半條魚了，如果運氣好，還能把這半條魚帶回去。不會的，他說，出海太遠已經把好運破壞了。

他大聲說：「別傻了，保持清醒，好好掌舵，也許還有很多好運在等著你。」

「如果有賣運氣的地方，我倒想去買一點。」他說。

我用什麼來買？他自問。我可以用丟掉的魚叉、斷成兩截的刀子，還有兩隻受傷的手去買嗎？

他說：「也許可以，你曾想用八十四天的討海日子來買運氣，他們也差一點賣給了你。」

他想，我不應該再胡思亂想了。運氣能以不同的面貌出現，誰能認得出來？他想，無論是什麼面貌，我都想買一些，決不討價還價。我想要的東西太多了，但此刻我希望能看到燈火的光。他盡量讓自己舒服一點，以便掌舵。他從疼痛中，知道自己還沒死。

大約晚上十點左右，他看到小鎮燈火所反射出的亮光。剛開始那些亮光猶如月亮初升時的光芒那樣微弱，接著隔著不斷增強的波濤和海風，亮光變得穩定清晰。老人朝亮光處駛去，他想，現在不用多久就會航行到溪岸的邊緣了。

他想，一切總算過去了。鯊魚可能會再來襲擊我，而一

個在黑暗中手無寸鐵的人,又能夠做什麼?

老人全身僵直酸痛,所有的傷口和用力拉傷的部位,在寒夜裡顯得格外疼痛難忍。他想,真希望不要再搏鬥了,多希望不用再搏鬥了啊。

可是,到了半夜,老人又和鯊魚開始戰鬥,他知道這次是毫無希望了。牠們成群結隊而來,老人只見牠們的鰭在水中劃出紋路,和撲上魚時身上所發出的燐光。他用棍棒打牠們的頭,聽到牠們嘴巴的咀嚼聲,還有牠們在船底下肆虐讓小船晃動不停的聲音。老人憑感覺和聲音拚命地打,他感覺有什麼東西抓住了棍子,然後棍子就不見了。

老人從船舵取下舵,拿著舵去打、去砍。他兩手握著舵,一次次往下打。但鯊魚群已經竄到船頭,一條接一條,成群簇擁而上。當牠們轉一圈再游回來時,他看見魚肉被撕得四分五裂,在海水下閃著亮光。

最後,有一條鯊魚撲過來搶食魚頭,老人知道這一次什麼都完了。他用舵對準了鯊魚頭打下去,鯊魚的嘴巴卡在沉重又撕不爛的魚頭上,他不斷揮打,聽到舵柄斷裂的聲音。他舉起斷裂的舵柄朝鯊魚戳去,他感覺已經刺進去,知道舵柄很尖利,他又戳了下去。鯊魚鬆了口,翻滾著游開。這是鯊魚群的最後一條,再沒有可供牠們吃的了。

老人這時幾乎喘不過氣來,嘴巴還有一股怪味道,帶點銅味,甜甜的,他擔心了一下,不過,味道還不是很重。

老人往海裡吐了口唾沫，說：「吃吧，虎鯊，你們大可去做一場好夢，夢到你們幹掉了一個人類。」

他現在知道，他最後已經被打敗了，而且無法補救。他走到船尾，發現半截的舵柄，還可以勉強拴在舵樺頭上供他航行。他把布袋放在肩上，把小船駛向航道。現在船駕起來輕鬆多了，他什麼都不想，對任何事也沒感覺。如今一切都已成過去，現在只有盡力駕船，好好地駛回小鎮的港口。深夜時，鯊魚又來吃食魚的殘骸，就好像有些人撿拾桌上的麵包屑一樣。老人不再理會牠們，除了掌舵外，對其他事都漠不關心。他只注意到小船旁沒有了沉重的負荷，航行起來多麼輕巧順利。

他想，小船仍然無恙，除了舵柄以外，一點損壞都沒有，而要更換舵柄是很容易的。

他可以感覺到現在已經航進海流中，而且能看見沿岸海灘上房子所透出的燈光。他知道自己在什麼地方，回家不成問題了。

他想，不管怎樣，風是我們的朋友，接著他又補充了一句，有時候是這樣沒錯。大海中有我們的朋友，也有我們的敵人。他想，床，床是我的朋友，就只有床，床真是一個好東西，當你被擊敗了，床會給你安慰。以前都沒想到床是這麼舒服。他想，到底是什麼東西把你打敗了？

他大聲說：「沒有人打敗我，是我自己出海太遠了。」

老人駛入小港時，露天酒店的燈光已經熄滅，他知道人們都入睡了。海風穩定地吹著，而且愈吹愈大。港灣靜悄悄的，老人把船靠向岩石下的一堆圓卵石上，沒人幫忙他，他只好獨力把船盡量往上拖。他下了船之後，把船繫在岩石上。

他卸下桅杆，把船帆捲起來捆好。然後，把桅杆扛在肩上，開始往上爬。這時候，他才知道自己有多累。他停下來一會兒，回頭一望，在街燈的掩映下，他看見那條大魚的大尾巴，挺立在船尾後。他看見牠光禿的背脊骨形成白色的線，還有牠黑漆漆的頭顱，前面伸出一根長喙，全身只剩下一副軀殼骨架。

　他再處開始往上爬，爬上頂端時，摔了一跤。他把桅杆
橫在肩上，躺在地上歇了一會兒。之後他想站起來，但站
不起來，便扛著桅杆坐在地上，望著馬路。一隻貓匆匆地
從遠處經過，老人看了一下，之後又望向馬路。

　最後，他放下桅杆站起來，然後再把桅杆扛在肩上，開
始上路。在走回小屋的一路上，老人坐下來休息了五次。

　走進小屋後，他把桅杆靠在牆上，在黑暗中摸到一個水
瓶，喝了口水，便倒在床上。他拉起毯子蓋住肩膀，再蓋
住背和腿，臉枕著報紙，雙臂伸直，手心朝上，睡著了。

　第二天早晨，小孩從門外朝屋子裡望時，老人酣睡未
醒。風刮得很大，停泊的船隻無法出海，所以小孩很晚才
起床，然後像以往一樣，每天早上醒後來便來老人的小

屋。小孩看著老人的呼吸，然後再看看老人的雙手，不禁開始流下了眼淚。他悄悄地走出去，去弄些咖啡來，一路上邊走邊哭。

很多漁夫圍在小船四周，觀看綁在小船旁的是什麼東西，其中有一個漁夫站在水中，捲起褲管，用一根繩子量魚骨的長度。

小男孩沒有下去看，他之前已經去過看了，有一個漁夫在幫他處理那艘小船。

「他還好吧？」一位漁夫喊道。

「睡著了，誰都不要去吵他。」小男孩叫道。他一點都不在意別人看見他在哭。

那個在量魚骨長度的漁夫叫道：「從鼻子到尾巴，足足有十八呎長。」

小男孩說：「我相信有那麼長。」

他到露天酒店要了一罐咖啡。

「熱的，多加些奶精和糖。」

「還要別的嗎？」

「不用了，等一下看他要吃什麼再說。」

老闆說：「好大的一條魚，從來沒看過那麼大的魚，你昨天釣到的兩條也很不錯。」

「去那兩條魚的。」小男孩說，然後又哭了起來。

「你要不要喝點什麼？」老闆問。

「不用了，叫他們不要去吵山帝亞哥，我會再來。」小男孩說。

「請轉達我的遺憾之情。」

「謝謝。」小孩回答道。

小男孩拿著熱咖啡罐來到老人的小屋，坐在他的旁邊，等他睡醒。有一次，他好像醒過來了，卻又沉沉睡去。小孩只好走到對街，借些柴火來熱咖啡。

老人終於醒過來了。

小男孩說：「不要坐起來，先喝這個。」他倒了一些咖啡在杯子裡。

老人接過杯子喝下去。

「馬諾林，牠們把我打敗了，牠們確實把我打敗了。」
老人說。

「牠沒有把你打敗，那條魚沒有把你打敗。」

「牠的確沒有打敗我，不過，後來卻把我打敗了。」

「彼得瑞克在看守小船和船具，你要怎麼處理魚頭？」

「讓彼得瑞克砍下做魚餌好了。」

「那根尖嘴呢？」

「你要的話就拿去。」

「我要。現在我們要計畫一下別的事情。」小男孩說。

「他們有去找過我嗎？」

「當然有，出動了海岸警衛，還用飛機搜救。」

「海洋太大，船太小，很難找。」老人說。他好高興，
終於能對著人講話，不必自言自語或是對著海講話。他
說：「我很想你。你捕到什麼了？」

「第一天捕到一條，第二天一條，第三天兩條。」

「好極了。」

「現在我們又可以一起捕魚了。」

「不行，我運氣不好，我再也不會走運了。」

「管他什麼運氣，我會帶來好運。」小男孩說道。

「你家人會怎麼說？」

「我才不管，昨天我捕到兩條魚，但從現在開始，我們

要一起去捕魚，我還有好多東西要學。」

「我們得弄一個鋒利的長矛，固定放在船上。你可以
去舊福特車上去找個鋼板彈簧，做成刀子，拿到哥拿巴客
那裡去磨利，不能用火燒，那很容易斷。我的刀子已經斷
了。」

「我會把鋼板彈簧磨利，也會另外弄把刀子來。強風還
要刮幾天？」

「大概三天，也可能更久一點。」

「我會把一切準備就序，你老人家先把手治療好再說。」小男孩說。

「我知道要怎樣把手治好。昨天晚上，我吐了一些奇怪的東西，胸口好像要裂開一樣。」

「把胸口也調養好，您老人家先躺下來，我替你拿件乾淨的襯衫來，再弄點東西給你吃。」小男孩說。

老人說：「我不在時的報紙，也順便帶一份過來，隨便哪一天都可以。」

「你一定要快快好起來，我要學的東西還很多，你樣樣都可以教我。你吃了不少苦頭吧？」

「好多。」老人說。

小男孩說：「我去把食物和報紙帶來，你老人家好好休息，我去藥房替你拿點擦手的藥。」

「不要忘記告訴彼得瑞克，我要把魚頭給他。」

「我會記得的。」

小男孩走出門，沿著碎珊瑚礁的路上走去，又忍不住哭了出來。

那天下午，露天酒店來了許多觀光客，朝海水望去。在空啤酒罐和死的梭魚之間，有一個女人看見一根又長又大的白脊骨，和一個很巨大的尾巴。東風在港外的海水上掀起波濤，尾巴隨著潮水起伏漂動。

「那是什麼？」她指著大魚的長背脊骨，問酒店的侍

者。現在魚骨頭已經變成垃圾，等著潮水把它沖走。

「大鯊魚。」侍者回答，想說說事情的經過。

「我不知道鯊魚這麼漂亮，牠尾巴的形狀很漂亮。」

「我也不知道。」她的男伴說。

沿著這條路上去的小屋裡，老人又入睡了。他仍是趴著睡，小男孩坐在他旁邊守候著。老人正夢見了獅子。

國家圖書館出版品預行編目資料

老人與海（原著雙語彩圖本）(The Old Man
and the Sea) / 海明威（Ernest Hemingway）
著；黛孜 譯. —初版. —[臺北市]：寂天文化,
2015.12　面；公分.

ISBN　978-986-318-070-8 (25K平裝)
ISBN　978-986-318-408-9 (25K精裝)

874.57　　　　　　　　　　　104025729

作者 _ 海明威（Ernest Hemingway）

譯者 _ 黛孜

校對 _ 陳慧莉

插畫 _ Julina Alekcangra

封面設計 _ 林書玉

製程管理 _ 洪巧玲

出版者 _ 寂天文化事業股份有限公司

電話 _ +886-2-2365-9739

傳真 _ +886-2-2365-9835

網址 _ www.icosmos.com.tw

讀者服務 _ onlineservice@icosmos.com.tw

出版日期 _ 2016年12月 初版再刷（250103）

郵撥帳號 _ 1998620-0 寂天文化事業股份有限公司

訂購金額600（含）元以上郵資免費

訂購金額600元以下者，請外加郵資65元

若有破損，請寄回更換